DAY ANOTHER PARADISE IN

by Robert Rahula

Day Another Paradise In

www.robertrahula.com

This is a work of fiction. Characters, organizations, businesses, products, locales, and events portrayed in this book either are products of the author's imagination or are used fictitiously.

First Printing, 2019

ISBN 978-1-7329708-2-3

Alma-Gator Press

Barcelona · Madrid · La Chorrera

for Caroline

Ah! Can it be
we have lived our lives
in a land of dreams?
—Oscar Wilde

Chapter 1:   The Day in Question

On the day in question, Ricardo, as was his custom, stopped by to see the old man and brought the usual bottle of Sangria for him. Sangria was the cheapest wine one could buy in Villa Rosario. The supermercado sold it in one-liter plastic bottles for the equivalent of four U.S. dollars. But the old man liked it.

Villa Rosario was a small town in Panama with a central park, two churches, one supermercado, and a smattering of restaurants and bars, all within walking distance of each other. The old man, however, lived about ten minutes outside of town, up on a hill. Ricardo hiked up to the old man's door and knocked. The old man yelled at him to come in.

"Cómo estás, mi amigo?" asked Ricardo as he entered.

The old man smiled and answered in Spanish, "Well, I've been seeing bats flying around outside my door, and I haven't even started drinking yet. I thought they were bats at first by the way they zigzagged left and right, then I thought maybe they were big birds, but then I decided it was The Giant Fly they put inside my eye."

The old man talked about The Giant Fly often. He said it lived inside his right eye and danced back and forth right in front of him whenever he looked at something plain, like a light-colored wall or a blue cloudless sky. He had described it once to Ricardo, saying it looked like some kid had twisted up a bunch of thin wires to look like a fly, with two giant eyes and a body, and long spindly legs that dangled down as it floated across this vision. The old man said that no matter where it floated in the room, it always turned to look at him, not with a menacing look, but with almost a friendly look. Sometimes, the old man confided once, the fly even talked to him.

One time, months before the day in question, in an effort to humor the old man, Ricardo had asked him, "Does it buzz?"

The old man had given Ricardo a disapproving look. "Of course not. It's inside my eye, floating in thick fluid. How could it buzz?"

"Oh, right," Ricardo had replied.

Jumping ahead from the day in question...a few months later, Ricardo was helping the old man organize his medical papers. A new medical clinic had opened in Villa Rosario. When the old man enrolled, they asked for all his medical records. The old man was a hoarder and had boxes of medical records. As Ricardo was placing the various reports, bills, receipts, etc., in chronological order, he came across a surgery report.

"You had a laser capsulectomy done on your right eye." Ricardo said to the old man as he looked at the report.

"Yes, I know," said the old man. "I was there when it happened."

Ricardo looked for a date on the report. "When was that done?"

"About five years after my cataract operation."

Ricardo thumbed through the document. "You went to Panama City for that?" he asked, looked at the address of the laser clinic.

"Well," said the old man, "you might have noticed that Villa Rosario is not exactly overrun with laser surgeons."

Ricardo laughed. One of the things he liked about the old man was his acerbic wit.

"The reason I was asking was because I was wondering if it was after that operation that The Giant Fly appeared."

The old man furrowed his brow and looked up, left and right, trying to remember. "I don't know..." he said. "Maybe."

"Well," said Ricardo, "maybe the fly is just a piece of tissue from the capsule, from when they lasered it off the back of your cataract lens. That happens sometimes, you know."

"Uh huh," said the old man. "That's the same thing the doctor said, but I know a Giant Fly when I see one."

"Oh," said Ricardo, "of course," and went back to organizing the files. That was the thing about the old man. You never knew if he was eccentric, crazy, or just fucking with you.

But returning to the day in question...the old man was saying thank you for the wine, as Ricardo handed him the bottle of Sangria. "I'll get some ice. Would you like a glass?"

"No, gracias," Ricardo said. "Actually, tonight I can only stay for a few minutes. I have to get home. I promised Carolina I would Skype with her tonight about her job."

"Ah, yes," said the old man, returning from the kitchen with a glass full of ice. "The beautiful Carolina. Why don't you bring her over tonight and you two can Skype right here and I can watch?"

Ricardo snorted, "You know she lives in the States. I can Skype with her, but I can't teleport her here."

"Well, you should bring her by sometime, at least. I want to see the beautiful Carolina again before I die."

"See her again? You've never seen her," Ricardo said.

"Well," the old man replied, as he filled his glass with Sangria, "that only underscores my point. I want to see the beautiful Carolina at least once before I die." The old man glanced at Ricardo slyly. "Tell me, don Ricardo, is she a panther in bed?"

"I wouldn't know," Ricardo said, "I've never slept with her."

"What!? Well, why are you wasting my time with these virgins? I am not young! I do not have time to break a new one in."

"Knock it off and drink your wine," Ricardo said. "Tonight is serious. She is having trouble at work and wants to talk. I need to be home in twenty minutes."

"What does she do?"

"She's a social worker for DSHS, a state agency that deals with poor people and their families."

"Well, then she's fucked," announced the old man. "If it's one group that DSS screws over more than the poor, it's their own workers."

"It's D-S-H-S. Do you even know what DSHS stands for, or what they do?"

"Nope," said the old man. "Don't need to. If it's a government agency and if it tries to help the poor, then it's in the business of fucking over everyone."

"Well, you may be right about that," Ricardo said. "They're trying to force her to falsify reports so they can take some kid away from its mom. They're telling her that if she won't do it, they'll fire her."

"They'll fire her anyway! Whether she does what they want or not."

"Why do you say that?" Ricardo asked.

"Because if she's complaining to you, then she's complaining to people at the job, and if she's complaining to people at work, then the bureaucratic bosses at DSS will hear of it. And if it's one thing that bureaucracies can't stand, it's a complainer. They'll put up with incompetence, stupidity, and negligence... but they'll *never* put up with a complainer, no matter how good a worker she might be. When she complains, she draws attention to her unit, and that threatens the other incompetent, stupid workers, and especially the incompetent and stupid bosses. They'll force her out, just like they're doing to her now. She needs to find another job."

"Well, that's what I thought," Ricardo said. "She says she wants to talk with a lawyer about suing."

"Ha," the old man grunted. "She won't win. They'll smear her and say her job performance was sub-par. Government organizations only exist to protect themselves. They pay lip service to whatever good idea originally spawned them. But once spawned, they are like rich people—their only interest is to protect their lifestyle. There are no market forces that hold them accountable."

"I didn't know you were an economist," Ricardo said.

"I'm not. I'm just old, and I've seen it all." The old man took a long swig of the Sangria from his glass. "Ah, that's good," he said approvingly. "Tell me, don Ricardo, I seem to recall that she got fired from her last job."

"That's true," said Ricardo.

"Ever notice, how some patterns repeat over and over in some people's lives?"

Ricardo sensed he was about to be pulled into another one of the old man's philosophical ramblings which, normally, he loved. But tonight, he was feeling anxious to get back to his apartment so that he could keep his Skyping appointment with Carolina. "Yes, I know," he answered in as neutral a tone as he could muster.

"Ever wonder why that is?" the old man continued. "Hmmm?"

"Yes, well..." Ricardo started to say, but the old man interrupted him.

"People say it's because of karma...but they don't understand karma. The Hindus believe it's because of unfinished business, that we are reincarnated to finish some issue in our lives. In a psychological sense, they are correct, except that the unfinished business is from our childhood, not our previous life. Anyway, the Hindus believe we have to keep trying to... to... to crack the nut as it were, to work through this issue, this unresolved pattern, until we get it right, so we keep being reborn as a person who is in that exact same situation."

"Are you sure that's the Hindus?" Ricardo asked.

"Hindu, Schmindu. It doesn't matter. The point is, I don't believe in all that reincarnation business."

"Then why did you bring it up?" Ricardo asked.

"So I could tell you what I *do* believe."

"Oh, of course...look, I do want to hear this, but I really have to go," Ricardo said as he stood up.

"Just let me tell you this one thing, and then you can go," the old man said.

"Okay," Ricardo said, and sat back down.

"The real reason that people repeat the same patterns over and over again, is because they have unresolved issues," the old man said. "Like I was saying, the Hindus were right about that part... but the unresolved issues are with their parents, or with their siblings, or both. But because those conflicts are unresolved, people keep seeking out other people to play those parts, like little psychodramas. So the rebel kid seeks out authoritarian bosses to rebel against, and the victim seeks out other bullies, and the control freak searches for uncontrollable partners... we just keep repeating these same patterns until we die."

"Yeah, yeah, I've heard you argue that before," Ricardo said. "That old Freudian crap of yours."

The old man chuckled. "You just don't agree with it because you think people can change!"

"Well, yes, that's true," Ricardo said. "I do think that."

"Well, you're *wrong*, don Ricardo. Nobody can change," the old man announced.

"Okay. But I really do have to go," said Ricardo. "I'll come back tomorrow, and we can talk more about this."

"Bring wine," the old man said.

"I always do," said Ricardo.

*   *   *

Earlier on the afternoon of the day in question, before Ricardo bought the wine to take to the old man, he was riding the bus back home to Villa Rosario from La Chorrera. The bus ride was usually thirty to forty minutes long, depending on traffic, but it was always a pleasant one, with the bus rolling through the lush green Panamanian countryside on relatively smooth roads. Ricardo found himself deep in thought. Carolina had emailed him earlier that morning with her story of persecution at DSHS and had asked him to Skype that night. Ricardo was thinking about her on the bus and feeling worried. One of the disadvantages to being an expat in another country was that when people you cared about were suffering back in the States, you were powerless to help them. Carolina was someone that Ricardo cared about. It was true, as he was to tell the old man later that night, that he had never slept with Carolina. He had wanted to since he first met her years ago, of course. But she was half his age and always had boyfriends her own age.

14

As such things happen, the sex simply never materialized. Timing, circumstance, and luck are still the most influential factors for any physical relationship. "Propinquity," the old man was fond of saying, "is everything." Still, Carolina was the kind of woman one could care about, even love, even though there was no sex. Such women were rare, at least as far as Ricardo had experienced. He had only known one other such woman in his life—his friend Marta back in New York. But he had not seen Marta for almost eight years now. They still emailed each other frequently, but the visits had become non-existent. She had moved to California, taken a new job and gotten married. As married people seemed to do, she had developed a new more insulated life. Gradually the in-person visits had become more difficult to schedule. Emails were still good, but Ricardo could feel Marta slowly drifting out of his life. With Carolina, Ricardo still was able to visit with her every time he traveled back to the States.

As the bus rumbled through the hills, Ricardo thought about love. He thought about all the women he had loved. Their names and faces and bodies danced before him. He remembered the old man had told him once: "Reminiscing is an old man's indulgence. The only warmth we have left is the comfort we take in reliving our memories of love. Memories of places leave us cold, but memories of warm thighs and wet pussies possess a small remnant of heat, and it pleases us to think of them. Sometimes it's all we have left." Ricardo liked the image of a memory holding a bit of heat.

But he did not like the thought that there might not be other lovers in his future. He tried to think of lovers in the past few years whose memory still held some heat. There was Magali, of course, but those embers were barely warm. Then he thought about Ali. Yes, that memory still glowed. But that affair was over two years ago. That is not to say there hadn't been regular sex over the past few months. The nearby city of La Chorrera had its share of brothels and bathhouses, but sex with strangers is, as everyone knows, different than sex with a lover.

"Whatever happened to that alley cat?" the old man

had asked him recently. Alley cat was the old man's nickname for Ali.

"Oh, I don't know. She got involved with some married dude who had money and connections, and she kinda drifted away."

"You didn't go after her?" the old man asked.

"No.... no, I never do that," Ricardo said.

"You are not willing to fight for a woman?"

"No," Ricardo said, "no, I'm not. I hate that whole competition bullshit."

"Hmm...well, it does make them feel important," the old man said, and then dropped the subject.

The truth was that Ricardo never did pursue women. When he was younger and arguably more handsome, it wasn't an issue. Women fell into his life like autumn leaves on a sidewalk. But as he had gotten older, he noticed that there were simply fewer women available to him. That is to say, fewer women whom he was attracted to were available to him. He would have no problem finding someone his own age, he presumed. But he preferred women who were fit and youthful in spirit. They did not have to be as young as Carolina, but they had to be fit. Most of the women his own age, for many sad reasons, had given up, grown heavy and dull, and lumbered through their days in acquiescence to old age.

The bus had stopped, to let some cattle cross the road. Ricardo was sitting near the front and he could see the cows slowly make their way across the road, their udders swaying back and forth. Two farmers with switches were trying to hurry them across the road so the bus driver would not start honking and scare them. "Women are cattle," the old man had told him once. "That's how society treats them. Raised only for breeding and then discarded." Ricardo could not disagree with the old man. He knew how pervasive the cultural view of women was, both in Panama and in the States. He thought that even his own preference for younger, fitter women was probably culturally engineered. It was amazing to Ricardo that evolution, that mechanism that was supposed to produce a superior creature in a superior

16

species, produced such a crappy, flawed malicious product as a human being. Ricardo didn't know it then, but later that night, when the old man was talking about how all state agencies only protected themselves, Ricardo would think back to his bus ride and recall his cynical view of what evolution had produced: a creature instinctively wired to lie, cheat, manipulate and destroy with no remorse.

The farmers got their cattle across the road, and the bus started up again. Ricardo thought back to his day so far: the early morning flurry of emails from Carolina, his bus ride into La Chorrera, his conversation with Miguel at the bathhouse, and now the ride back to Villa Rosario.

Ricardo had known Miguel for many years. In fact, they had originally met at a bathhouse when Ricardo had first moved to Panama. Miguel was one of two brothers-in-law who owned the Los Cuñados restaurant in La Chorrera. Although Miguel was married with two children, he was gay. For family and business reasons, of course, he kept himself deep in the closet. But once a week or so, he would meet Ricardo at the bathhouse and they would alternately cruise the darkened steam room together or sit and just talk about life.

Earlier on this particular day, they were sitting naked in the hot tub together, talking about Miguel's frustration with trying to get some workers to repair one of the large ovens in the restaurant's kitchen.

"It is so frustrating, don Ricardo," Miguel was saying. "They promised to come on Monday but didn't show up until Wednesday. I told them I needed the stove repaired before Friday because we needed it for the busy weekend. They promised it would be done by Thursday. Then they disappeared. I finally had to pay extra to have someone come in from Panama City with the correct parts. Luckily, they got it working by noon Friday."

"What happened to the first workmen?" Ricardo asked.

"I never saw them again," exclaimed Miguel. "They even left a few of their tools there, but never came back. And this is a common problem in my business, don Ricardo.

Someone promises to deliver something, like fresh fish, or promises to print new menus by a certain date, and it never happens on time! I love my customers, and I'm a good cook. But the restaurant business is just one ongoing headache. Sometimes I don't even know why Spanish has a future tense. People use it—they say, "I'll be here tomorrow at 9:00 sharp." But they never keep their commitment. It's as if the future tense is totally useless, totally beyond their grasp."

Ricardo laughed. "That would be interesting. A language with no past tense and no future tense... just a present tense... everything would just be here and now, no tomorrow, no past."

"Well, that's how it is with trying to get anything done here," Miguel said. "You know, my friend, Spanish has fourteen different tenses. It's a complicated language. But it's as if the tenses have no meaning. If it's not something that needs to be done right now, it just doesn't get done."

Just then a young man walked by the hot tub, glanced at Miguel and Ricardo and gave them a little smile, and then stepped through the door that led to the steam room.

"Do you think it's time we take a little stroll, my friend?" Miguel asked.

"I was just thinking the same thing," said Ricardo.

They both stepped out of the hot tub, grabbed their towels and entered the steam room.

The memory of him and Miguel entering the steam room and finding the young man waiting for both of them brought a smile to Ricardo as the bus continued its drive to Villa Rosario. The bus turned off the main paved road and started making its way slowly over a dirt road that marked the last mile into Villa Rosario. He and Miguel had played with the young man in the dark steam room for a while, and then the three of them went to one of the small rooms with a bed in the back of the bathhouse and closed the door. The bus bounced up and down over the pot-holed road, and the feeling seemed to be in rhythm with Ricardo's memory of that afternoon's threesome with Miguel and the young man. What a strange life this is, Ricardo thought, that some physical acts that only happen in darkened rooms can have such a natural grace and beauty.

He remembered one time when the old man asked him about it. "Why do you waste your time at the bathhouse?" the old man had asked.

"Well," Ricardo explained, "I guess it's because it's convenient. Everyone is there for the same thing. You don't have to talk about it. You don't have to beat around the bush. Everyone is polite. Sometimes you have to wait for the right person to come along with the right chemistry. But usually, there's someone. I rarely spend more than two hours there before I find someone cute to have sex with."

"Ah, yes...thighs without faces. And how do you know you are safe?" the old man asked.

"I only play safe," Ricardo said. "It's the only way."

"Many people there do not play safe," the old man said.

"How would you know?" Ricardo asked.

"I am just old, and I've seen it all," replied the old man, his standard answer for any time Ricardo questioned one of his assertions.

"But you should find a lover, someone you can trust, and build an actual relationship," the old man continued.

"Well, I would if I could. It's not that easy. I'm no spring chicken myself," Ricardo replied.

"You aren't trying hard enough."

"I'm not trying at all," Ricardo said. "It is not my nature to try. I will wait until someone comes into my life."

"You should try 'date-latina-women-now-dot-com'. I get all the sex I want from that dating site," the old man said.

"You are such a bullshitter," Ricardo replied. "You don't belong to any dating sites."

The old man smiled. "Probably not," he said. "But you never know."

The bus stopped at the only stop in Villa Rosario, in the center of town near the Parque Central and the Catholic Church. Luckily, Ricardo's apartment was only a few blocks away. On the walk home, Ricardo stopped and bought a bottle of Sangria for the old man for later that evening, but he thought he would take a short nap first before going to see him.

Chapter 2:   Skype

It was still early evening on the day in question when Ricardo got back to his apartment from his brief visit with the old man and began his Skype session with Carolina. Since he was attempting to reach her from Panama, it usually took a few attempts to connect to her Skype account. This night was no different. Eventually he got through, and there she was on his computer screen, sitting in her bedroom back in the States. Normally she was smiley and chatty, but tonight she looked worried, launching straight into her story about work. She told him that they hadn't fired her yet, but that she knew it was coming. She just could not go through being fired again, so she was working on a letter of resignation. She read her first draft out loud to Ricardo.

"Based on the incidents of the Wilson case, wherein you demanded that I engage in unprofessional and unethical conduct by falsifying a petition to terminate parental rights, I am hereby tendering my letter of resignation," she read. "I simply cannot continue to work in such a hostile environment that fosters this type of illegal activity. As you are well aware, I pointed out during several staff meetings that the facts of this case simply do not meet the statutory standards for filing a petition. I consulted with the Office of the Attorney General, and they agreed with me. Yet you threatened to fire me if I did not draft what was clearly a false petition. I consider this illegal retaliation and will be seeking legal counsel... Well, that's it, Ricardo. What do you think?"

Ricardo took a deep breath and said, "The letter is good. I might make a few changes... but before I get into that, let me back up and ask you a few threshold questions. Have you talked to a union rep about this at all?"

"Met with them twice," Carolina said. "They were

pretty useless. They told me that the department has the legal authority to decide when to file a petition, and that they could order me to draft the petition. If the department later got into trouble for it, the agency would be liable, not me."

"Uh huh..."

"But, the fact is, Ricardo, my name would be on it. The lies they want me to write would be under my name. People would think I did it, regardless of who was legally liable."

"Oh, I understand, Carolina, I understand. And what about this meeting with the AG that you referred to?"

"Well I called them the other day and explained the situation. They agreed with me that the petition was bullshit, but their position was that their job is simply to go to court and defend the petition. If the Wilson family gets a lawyer and fights it, the Assistant AG I talked to said that the agency would lose the case in court. But you know how that is... these families can't afford to hire a lawyer, and the kid would be taken away from them for weeks before they got a court hearing, and I'd be the one called as a witness to defend why I wrote the petition. The AG actually suggested I file the petition and then tell the family to fight it. That way, the judge takes the blame for dismissing the petition. But that's so crazy Ricardo! I just won't do that. That family may not be the best family, but they're doing an okay job. I think the schoolteacher who called in the original complaint to DSHS just has it in for the mother and is using the agency to get revenge. It's sick."

"And what about staying at DSHS until you find another job?" Ricardo asked.

"I have been applying for other jobs for the past month. I had an interview last week that I think went well. But I'm out of time. They want me to file the petition tomorrow. And I'd rather quit than be fired."

"I understand. How's your money situation?"

"Well," Carolina said, "I think I have enough savings to last three months. I think I could find another job in that time."

Ricardo thought for a moment about how difficult it was to find a job when you're unemployed, and how that's often a focus point in any job interview. But he also could tell how frustrated and scared Carolina was. He didn't want to push it either way.

"So, as they used to say in that old game show: Is this your final answer? Or are you still in the decision-making process?" Ricardo asked.

"I guess I'm still on the fence. Clearly, I need to quit. I'm not exactly sure what I'm going to do tomorrow, but I wanted to have the letter ready."

"Okay, okay," said Ricardo. "Well, that answers my questions. Back to the letter. Take out the part about consulting with an attorney. You don't want to tip your hand. Besides, if for some reason someone higher up comes to their senses and wants to keep you, saying the word 'attorney' will stop them. And be sure to not mention the family's name in the letter. Use whatever initials or code they use to identify the file. And rather than hand them the letter, which can get conveniently lost, email it to them, with a copy to the regional administrator, the union, and a copy to yourself. That way the email is in their system. If at some point a year or two from now, anyone does a Freedom of Information request for all emails complaining of unethical supervision, they will have to turn over your email."

"Yeah, thanks, those are good points," said Carolina. "Why is life so hard, Ricardo?"

"It's just hard because you are young and you have ethics, my dear."

"Does it get easier?"

"No," said Ricardo. "You just get older."

"Ha," said Carolina. "How many years were you a lawyer?"

"Well, I started late. It was a second career for me. But I did it for about twenty years. It was all I could take."

Ricardo was quiet for a minute while he thought again about what it was like to be young and scared and fighting a bureaucratic system where you can't win.

"May I ask, Carolina, how much money you take

home each month from this job?"

"My take home pay? About $2500 a month."

"Hmm...well, listen, I don't have a lot of money, but if the job search lasts longer than three months, I can give you some money to get by on."

Now it was Carolina's turn to be quiet. Then she said, "I appreciate that. I think I'll be okay, but I appreciate that."

Chapter 3:   Power

Later that night, after the Skype session, Ricardo recalled a conversation he once had with the old man about the power dynamics that are always involved with women.

"Nah," the old man was saying. "Women got fucked on the money trip. They were doing fine until man invented the alphabet, then man used that to write up contracts and laws to fuck women over."

"What are you talking about?" asked Ricardo.

"The Giant Fly explained it all to me, how eons ago, women were considered magical beings because babies came out of them. Men were too stupid to realize that their little squirts of joy juice contained sperm. They thought women were magical, goddesses, divine creators of all life. And women used that to rule over men. It was a matriarchal world, and women had all the wealth and power. But then men conspired and created the alphabet and taught other men how to read and then told women that the gods had given them—the men—the alphabet, and then they forbade women to read, and they created ledgers and taxes and deeds and laws... and slowly they took all the power and all the wealth away from women."

"God, you are so full of shit," Ricardo said, refilling the old man's glass with Sangria and refilling his own glass as well.

"Well, look at the world. The politicians and the lawyers and the priests are all men."

"That's changing," Ricardo said, "except for maybe the priests."

"Okay, well look at the simple distribution of power in any male-female relationship," said the old man.

"Yeah," said Ricardo, "women have the power. They choose who to let into their bed."

"That's the only area where they still have power left," said the old man, but even then, if a man is rich, he finds himself invited into more beds."

"I've heard that's true," said Ricardo, "but I don't have any personal knowledge of that."

"Now it is you who is bullshitting, my friend. You are a gringo here. Even with only the Social Security check you live on down here, you make far more money than the locals. There are plenty of women here who would sleep with you for that alone."

"Yes, and I know exactly where they are," said Ricardo, "They're at Jenny's brothel."

"I'm not talking about prostitutes, don Ricardo. I'm talking about the flicker in a woman's eye when you are talking to her and she realizes that you are talking to her and that you are a gringo... You can see the wheels turn in her head, can you not? You have noticed that they are extra nice to you, even in the restaurants when they bring you food, or in the stores. They smile sweetly to you, do they not?"

"True," said Ricardo.

"That's the first step of the power differential. Because they perceive you as having wealth, they are immediately nicer to you at the first meeting, just in case a relationship might happen, which they want, because you have wealth."

"I don't have wealth," Ricardo protested.

"Here you do, relatively speaking," insisted the old man.

"Well, if they want me, I'm not aware of it. They never flirt with me," said Ricardo.

"That's cultural," said the old man, "Women here would not dare to flirt with you. They will be sweet; they will be nice; they will smile, but they will not flirt. It is you who must make the first move."

"Ha... well, that explains my lack of success," Ricardo said.

"Undoubtedly. You could have any woman you wanted down here, but you are a man, and men are stupid. We invented the alphabet and all the fancy poetic words of love, and ever since then, we have sat back and rested on our laurels. We don't even try anymore. If it wasn't for the fact that we used the alphabet to beat women down so much that they gave up, they would rise up and enslave us again. Eventually they will, of course, but not in my lifetime and not in yours either.

"And the fly in your eye told you all this?" Ricardo asked.

"Yup. Would you be so kind, don Ricardo, to get me some ice from the icebox?"

Ricardo got up and went into the old man's kitchen. As he was getting the ice, he noticed about ten small tacks on the counter, placed so that the sharp points faced up. He brought the ice tray back to the old man.

"What are all those tacks doing on your kitchen counter? Ricardo asked.

"Ah, that was another ingenious idea from The Giant Fly. When the ants come, I spray them and kill them. Then I take the tacks and carefully stab their tiny bodies and turn the tacks point up. That way, when the other ants come, and they see their comrades impaled on the metal stakes, hanging there like tiny crucified Jesuses, they will become very scared and run away."

The old man reached in to the tray and took several ice cubes and dropped them in his wine. "Thank you, don Ricardo."

Ricardo stared at him for a minute, shook his head and took the ice tray back to the icebox. Then he looked closely at the tacks. It was true. At the top of each one was a small black clump. Ricardo would not have noticed it had not the old man told him. He bent over and looked closely. It did look like there was a tiny ant impaled on the top of each tack.

Ricardo went back to the living room and sat down and said, "You know, I think you are truly insane."

The old man laughed. "True," he said, "but I haven't seen an ant since I put the tacks out."

* * *

Ricardo wasn't sure why this memory had come back to him on the evening of the day in question, after his Skype conversation with Carolina, except that he felt that she was being crucified for following her ethics. It made him sad, because one of the things he loved about her was that she was such an ethical person. But for some reason, she was always getting fucked over because of it. He remembered the last job she had, before she joined DSHS, where she was doing social work for some Catholic organization. One of the families she was working with had a fifteen-year- old daughter whom the father had gotten pregnant. The girl didn't want to have the baby and had asked Carolina how she could get an abortion. Carolina simply told her that the local Planned Parenthood organization had counselors on staff and performed legal abortions. Carolina knew that her employer forbade her from advocating abortion. But it was simply common knowledge that Planned Parenthood existed and that their clinics would perform free abortions for under-aged victims of rape. But just for saying that much, Carolina was fired from her job.

Ricardo remembered the conversation he had with her at the time. "You know," he told her, "I think they were trying to make an example out of you."

"But I didn't do anything wrong," she said.

"Of course you didn't. I'm proud of what you did. But you gave them the opportunity to use you to make a political point."

"But it's not fair! That girl was raped."

"Fairness has nothing to do with it, my dear. It wasn't fair that they crucified Jesus, or imprisoned the protesters at Tiananmen Square, or hung Nathan Hale, or convicted John Scopes... but they did, and they got away with it. You've *got* to learn to think more politically. If you want to influence someone in a political system, you have to do it indirectly. You should have gotten some friend, who didn't work with you at the organization, to give the information to the girl, so you'd have plausible deniability."

"But I'm not allowed to tell people outside the organization about confidential cases. That's an ethical violation in itself," Carolina said.

"That's not an ethic—that's just a convenient rule for the organization. Besides, even if it was an ethical violation, you can't let one set of ethics hamstring a higher ethic. We live in a political world, Carolina. *Everything* is political."

These memories about Carolina ran through Ricardo's mind after the Skype session, as he sat at his desk and thought about her and how rough her tomorrow was going to be. He hoped that things would work out for her. It was getting late, but he wasn't sleepy. He had taken a long nap before going to see the old man, had slept hard and had had a strange dream. He tried to remember it, but all he could recall were images. It had something to do with him being back in the States. It was Christmastime, except that Christmas ornaments and icons were floating through the air everywhere he went. He was standing in a coffee shop in the dream, and the air was full of floating silver scarves and red Christmas tree balls and Christmas cards. He had to swish them away like large insects in order to get his coffee from the girl at the counter and sit at a table. Then some woman he knew named Chrissy came walking in through the door, and Ricardo was trying to wave at her and get her attention, but all the objects kept floating between him and her. That was all he could remember.

"Dreams," the old man had told him one time, "don't mean shit. All that dream interpretation stuff is just bullshit."

"What do you think they are then?" Ricardo had asked.

"Well, let me explain," said the old man. "As you fall asleep, your mind descends. It actually goes down through the various layers of consciousness as it falls toward the lowest level, which is lack of consciousness, or sleep. And as it passes through these various levels of consciousness, it picks up different memories, like dust particles, that just stick to your mind. They're just random thoughts and images that float in different layers of consciousness. So you fall asleep, and collect all these images, this memory dust, and then the same thing happens when you wake up. You mind ascends and picks up more random images and memories. And when you wake up, your poor brain has to make sense out of all this memory dust that it's coated with, like pollen stuck to the legs of honeybees. That's all dreams are, just random crap your mind is throwing up, like dust particles on the road. Now, that's different from intuition. Intuition is important, especially when it comes and tells you to be careful. And sometimes intuition comes to you just when you are waking up. But it feels different...and it has a different voice. It's not like a dream image. In fact, intuition is often without images. It comes as a fact, or a warning. But dreams just are phantoms, memory dust."

"And how do you know this?" Ricardo asked.

"I'm just old and I've seen it all," said the old man.

"Oh yeah, right," said Ricardo. "I forgot."

Chapter 4: The Dream

Although Ricardo did not remember it, what really happened in the dream was this:

He was in a coffee shop. It was long and narrow, with five small booths inside next to a large glass window. There were more tables outside. Opposite the tables was a glass counter full of pastries and breads. Behind that was the bakery, staffed by several bakers and assistants. Ricardo was correct about the air, however. It was full of floating Christmas ornaments, Christmas cards, and for some reason, long silver scarves. They floated around slowly, as if they were moving in a thick vitreous fluid. But it was just air. Ricardo brushed them aside while he waited his turn to order food. The long silver scarves were the most annoying, because they would brush against his face and give off small silver particles that also floated in the air.

He got to the counter, pushing aside several floating ornaments and Christmas cards, and pointed to some apple danishes. Although he couldn't hear any words being spoken, he knew that he told the girl behind the counter that he wanted two of the danishes and a cup of coffee. She got the pastries, put them on a small white plate, too small for the large pastries in fact, and also got him a cup of coffee and placed them both on the counter. He couldn't understand how much money she wanted so he handed her a ten dollar bill and she rung the order up and handed him some change. He took the plate and the cup of coffee and walked over and placed them on one of the vacant tables. Then he went to a side table by the counter and got a napkin, a fork, a spoon, and several packets of artificial sweetener. He returned to his table, brushing away several floating scarves, sat down, poured the sweetener into the coffee and stirred it.

31

Just then he saw Chrissy come in the front door. He was sitting about two booths away from the front door, facing it. But there were several ornaments and scarves floating in the air between them, and Chrissy did not see him.

Chrissy was a woman Ricardo had worked with at one time. She was skinny, almost anorexic, with shoulder length blonde—almost white-blond—hair, and very pale skin. She usually wore long-sleeved blouses that buttoned all the way up to her neck. The material was often soft and clung to her body, and Ricardo had often enjoyed watching her move when he used to see her at work, enjoying the way he could make out the swelling of her breasts and the lines of her bra. He loved imagining what her breasts looked like and envisioned them having very pink nipples. Even the long dresses she wore at work clung to her legs and outlined them all the way up.

Chrissy was making her way up to the counter. She still had not seen Ricardo. He started to raise his hand to wave at her. That's when time split in two, right in front of his eyes. On the left side of his field of vision, he could see one future, as she walked up to the counter without seeing him, and ordered some pastries to go. In that vision, he did not wave to her, did not call to her. She paid for the pastries and walked out of the coffeeshop without ever seeing him. On the right side of his field of vision, an alternative future was unfolding. In that future, he was standing up, waving his arms in a crisscross fashion, and calling out to her, although there was no sound. She saw him and came up and sat down at his table and was looking at him about to say something.

Ricardo had the distinctive feeling in the dream, as he watched the two futures playing out in front of him, that he had the ability to choose which future would happen. It was also clear that the future to his left would be a future like his past, that is, not taking any action, but letting things unfold, whereas the future on the right would be a new, and hence risky, behavior for him, i.e., calling attention to himself, initiating contact, being bold and direct.

But the thing that was most intense about the dream was the strong physical attraction he was feeling toward

Chrissy. He knew very little about her, had rarely spoken to her at work, but the visual history of always watching her clothes cling to her body excited him, and made him want to tear off those long sleeved blouses and see the rest of her pale white body.

So there Ricardo sat, watching the two futures, just on the verge of choosing, when the dream ended. Ricardo continued to sleep and would awaken approximately ten minutes later remembering only a few fragmented images from the dream.

The old man was half-right. What we remember about dreams *is* nonsense, total nonsense. But if we could remember the whole dream, we would know that they are perfect psychological pictures of our existential state of being, complete gestalts unto themselves, exact blueprints of our desires and inhibitions. But it never happens that we can remember the whole dream. Even when we think we do, we don't. It simply never happens.

Chapter 5:   Email

After Ricardo woke up from his nap and the half-remembered dream, he got up and went to the kitchen to reheat a half cup of coffee left over from the morning pot. Then, he started thinking about Marta. Somehow, thinking about Carolina, earlier on the bus ride back from La Chorrera, had reminded Ricardo how much he cared about Marta, what a good person she was, and how important she had once been in his life. It had been several weeks since he had sent her an email, so he sat at his desk and wrote one:

"It's been a quiet week here, Marta. Not much news. I'm going to go see that old man I told you about tonight. I've grown rather fond of him. He's crazy as a loon, but he makes me laugh. I usually take him a bottle of wine, and we sit and talk for an hour or so, although I won't have time to visit long with him tonight because I promised my friend Carolina I would call her. But I bought a bottle of wine this afternoon and I'll take it to him tonight anyway. He won't mind, because it'll be more for him to drink. And I'll see him tomorrow night. But I'll give you an example of how crazy he is. The other day we were talking about science. I think it came up because I was saying I was so bad at science in school, or something like that...and out of the blue he asked me whether I thought there could be gravity without mass. And I thought about it for a bit, and I said no, that I thought you had to have mass to create gravity, like the mass of the earth that creates the gravity that holds us, or the mass of the sun that keeps the earth spinning around it. But he said—and this was the crazy thing—that he'd been thinking *a lot* about it recently, and he had decided that there was, in fact, gravity without mass. He said that gravity had nothing to do with mass. He said that gravity just exists and that mass somehow just bends it and creates the impression that there's a gravitational field around the mass. He kept insisting that gravity was like the stretchy material of a trampoline and mass was like a bowling ball in the middle of the trampoline. And so I asked him how mass was able to bend gravity, and he looked at me as if I was stupid and said because it was heavy. So, we got into this argument, and I said that there is no weight in space, and he said of course there is, it's just measured differently. I asked him how it was measured, and he said that everything was connected by these invisible strings and that the heavier objects pulled on the strings... Anyway, that's the type of conversation I have with this dude all the time. He's just a hoot.

"In other news... well, there's really not much. I went to La Chorrera and saw my old friend Miguel today. And as I mentioned, I'm going to Skype with Carolina tonight. You remember her? She's the one who originally convinced me to visit Panama oh so many years ago. Anyway, she's having problems at work and wants to talk.

"But I was thinking about you today and hoping you were doing well. And I realized how long it's been since we've actually seen each other, and that makes me sad. I'm planning to visit the States again in about three months, and I think it'll be a tour of the western states. Do you have any travel plans coming up? I'd sure like to see you again. Anyway, keep in touch. I always love hearing from you.

Love, Ricardo."

Not much of an email, he thought, but that's how it is when you haven't seen someone for a long time. There is simply less to build on. Still, Marta had been his best friend for so many years, so many years ago, that he would keep trying to stay in touch. He hit the Send button and closed his laptop. He checked his watch. He had time to stroll down to the Parque Central and get a bite to eat before he walked over to the old man's place.

He took the bottle of Sangria out of the freezer where he had placed it before his nap, wrapped it in a small towel, and placed it in his knapsack.

As he walked towards the Parque Central, Ricardo thought about the old man. Yes, what he had written to Marta was true: the old man was a hoot, and fun to talk with. But at times he could be exasperating. Ricardo recalled one time when the old man was ranting about free will, or more precisely, the lack of free will.

"There is no such thing as free will," the old man was saying. "It's just an illusion because we're stuck in time."

"Umm, that makes no sense. What do you mean?" asked Ricardo.

"Well," the old man explained, "in order to have free will, you have to have an undetermined future, that is, the choice you are making today with your so-called free will has to create the future. That's the whole idea around the concept of karma."

"Right..." said Ricardo, "but I still don't follow you."

"Well, if your future is fixed, if it's set, then you can't alter it," said the old man. "We think we're making a free choice, but we're not. We've already chosen. There is no future. It's already happened, or rather, it's already happened in the future. We just don't know it, because we're stuck in the Now. Our consciousness is just floating along a road that's already been paved. We're just sitting in the backseat seeing the scenery all for the first time and thinking it's all new."

"Oh, I see what you're saying," said Ricardo, a little disappointed. "The future is fixed, so we can't have free will, yada yada yada. It's an old argument."

"It's an old argument because it's true! When the gods got bored they created mankind and time. But time is not how we perceive it. The gods created time like we build roads. This road goes here and that road goes there. Just because you're traveling on it doesn't change where it's going. You can have all the free will you want, but if your car is on the road to Anton, you're going to Anton. And as for time, the gods only invented time so they could inhabit our bodies."

"What? Why would they want to do that?"

"So they could experience this illusion you call free

will," said the old man.

"You've lost me again," said Ricardo. "Why would they want to inhabit our bodies and experience time and free will if they already knew what the outcome was?"

"Ah ha!" exclaimed the old man. "That is the point of the game. They give themselves amnesia when they inhabit our bodies so that they forget they are gods.   Life is all a game to them. They wired it up so that when we're born we forget we're gods, and we don't remember until we die. Don't you see how it all fits?"

Ricardo looked carefully at the old man. "So... you're saying that we're all gods and we don't know it?"

"Exactly!" the old man beamed.

"You're nuts," Ricardo said.

"Really?" asked the old man. "Are you any better off for all your free will, don Ricardo? You were a lawyer in the States, no? You were a handsome young man, no? And yet, what happened? How many times did you say you were in rehab? How many marriages did you fuck up? How much money did you waste? You ended up here, in this piss-poor country, living alone in this pissant town because you can't afford to live anywhere else in the world. You can't sustain a relationship. You spend your time in bathhouses, brothels, and bars. You are old and you have wasted your life, your free will life. All the good choices you could have made, and each time you fucked it up. If your will is so free, why did you never use it? Why is it always out of reach? Huh? Tell me that, Mr. Smartypants lawyer."

"Oh fuck you!" Ricardo said.

"Really? Compare our two philosophies, don Ricardo. I am happy. You live a life of regret. Why? Because you think you made bad decisions. I didn't have to make any decisions, because my future was decided the day I was born. There was no decision for me to make, ever. I simply watched my life unfold. So I don't have to kick myself everyday for not making better use of my free will, because there is no free will, señor."

That conversation took place several months ago,

and Ricardo had stormed out of the old man's apartment that night and didn't go to see him for another week. But eventually, Ricardo decided that there was a bit of truth in what the old man had said, at least in terms of describing Ricardo's life. So after the anger subsided, Ricardo renewed his ritual of bringing the old man a bottle of wine and listening to his wild tales.

Ricardo thought about that conversation and the many others he had had with the old man as he walked to the Parque Central. He went to Soda de la Linda, a small three-table snack bar, and ordered a plate of chicken with rice and beans. Linda was the cook, waitress and owner. She had a grown son who ran a similar operation on the other side of the park. The menu was simple: rice and beans with your choice of chicken, pork, or beef. It wasn't much of a choice, but the food was cheap and good. Linda didn't talk much, but she nodded to Ricardo in recognition. Ricardo nodded back and said, "Casado con pollo, por favor."

He sat down and thought about Carolina, Marta, Miguel, and the old man. They represented his total circle of friends, his family now. Strange, he thought, how one's community shrinks as one gets older. He had heard of some old men who had lost their family and friends, one by one, dropping off to death or nursing homes until there was no one left. How strange, Ricardo thought, how strange it must be to have no friends at all, to know no one who knows you and your history. No one to sit and drink with and reminisce about the old days with. Ricardo thought it was like that old riddle about a tree falling in the forest. Do the good old days even exist if there is no one there to remember them? Maybe old men don't die from being tired; maybe they die from being lonely. If there's no one to share our achievements, our adventures, our dreams with, Ricardo thought, then they don't really exist. And if we are not our achievements, our adventures, and our dreams, what are we? It was a depressing thought.

Linda brought Ricardo a plate of food. "Fresca?" she said, asking him if he wanted a fruit drink. "Té frio," he replied, asking for iced tea.

39

Ricardo didn't want to end up without any friends. Yet it was he who had quit his job at the law firm in New York, moved to Panama, leaving behind all those circles of long-term acquaintances from which friends are often drawn. And yes, he had acquaintances down here in Panama, but he was a gringo. There was that subtle power divide, that uncrossable distance when you're a gringo. Only with Miguel had he managed to form a bond. But that was because Miguel needed friends who were supportive of his closeted gay life. Miguel wasn't a friend in the usual sense. Ricardo had never been to his house, nor met his wife and kids. He was only a part of Miguel's life as a customer in the restaurant and as a cruising partner in the bathhouse.

There was Jenny, the owner of the nicest brothel in La Chorrera. But theirs was a business relationship—respectful, but formal. And there was Magali, one of Jenny's employees. Ricardo had tried to develop a relationship with her. He had spent time with her outside of the brothel, and time with her in his bed, and it had been good, but there was that gringo thing again. Ricardo had had several relationships with different Panamanian women over the years, but eventually something would come up that highlighted the disparity of money: their kids would need new shoes, or they would need money for school, or their car would break down... and they simply never had any extra money, never any emergency funds. In every case, the gringo's cultural reflex is to offer to pay. You'd do it for a friend back in the States. Why wouldn't you do it here? Of course, the answer is that you never get your money back in Panama, because they don't have it, whereas your stateside friend would eventually repay you. And once you give the money to your Panamanian friend, the relationship is forever altered. The gringo becomes the well from where the water of life is drawn, where the money comes from for the next car repair, or the next pair of shoes.

Linda brought Ricardo's iced tea.

Ricardo had really liked Magali, and he tried to forestall the tainting of their relationship early on. He had sat her down and explained his theory of how money ruins relationships and he wanted a real relationship with her. He didn't mind that she was a prostitute for Jenny, because he knew that Jenny ran a clean place and insisted on safe sex practices. But if they were going to see each other outside of the brothel, then she could not bring up money issues. He would gladly pay for her meals if they went out to restaurants because he would do that for dates back in the States, but other than that, she had to pay her own way. She agreed to it, and for many months, things were good. But eventually, she came to him crying, asking for money. Ricardo didn't want to know why—it was something about her mother being sick—he simply gave her the money. But he knew it was over. The next time she asked him for money came soon after that, and he gave her that money too, but then broke up with her for good. She continued to work for Jenny. Ricardo simply asked Jenny not to bring her out when he went there. Jenny understood and would always offer him someone else when he went there.

Ricardo ate his meal in silence and thought about these things. A few minutes later, he finished, paid Linda, grabbed his knapsack and started to walk over to the old man's apartment.

Chapter 6:   Morning

On the morning of the day in question, hours before Carolina's email arrived, Ricardo was in a light sleep, lying on his side, just barely conscious of the morning light coming through the blinds. He wasn't aware of it, but he was snoring lightly. Somewhere in the distance outside some dogs were barking. Closer, in the trees outside his bedroom window, some birds were chirping to one another. It was the chirping sound that finally made its way into Ricardo's consciousness. He scratched his ear, turned his head to glance at the window shades to see how much light was coming into the room in order to judge what time it was, and guessed that it was about 6:30 a.m. He was off by about seven minutes. He stretched his naked body, kicked off the sheet, and went into the bathroom to pee.

Ricardo had always thought it was an interesting aspect to being a man, that the very first thing one encountered every morning was one's own cock. Because one invariably has to pee first thing every morning, being a man necessitates grabbing one's own cock and aiming the pee into the toilet. In essence, the first thing a man does every morning is touch himself. It was as if the urinary-genital system was designed to remind you immediately upon waking that you are a man.

Sometimes, depending on his early morning dreams, he would have a hard-on. He would still be able to pee, of course, but he had to bend slightly at the waist, and push his cock downward. If he was not hard, his cock would be relaxed and hanging low. He liked catching a glimpse of his naked body in the full length mirror on the bathroom door and seeing his cock first thing in the morning because it always looked bigger. During the day, of course, the stresses, tribulations, and general moving around would cause his cock to naturally pull up in protection and take on normal proportions. But in the morning, it had the appearance of being bigger, and that pleased Ricardo.

After peeing, Ricardo went into the kitchen to make coffee. He had placed a paper filter in the coffee maker the night before. He opened the refrigerator door and got the plastic container where he kept his coffee, removed the lid, and poured ground coffee into the paper filter. After returning the container to the refrigerator, he filled the coffee pot with water, poured that water into the coffee maker, put the coffee pot in its place in the machine, and turned the coffee maker on. Then he went back to bed, turned away from the light coming through the window, and tried to fall back to sleep.

The chirping and dripping of the coffee was a pleasant sound, and on many mornings Ricardo could drift back to sleep, but the hissing of the final drops of water turning into steam usually woke him up. And so it was this morning, on the day in question.

Ricardo got up again, poured a cup of coffee, added some sweetener, and went back to the bed. He placed his coffee cup on the table next to the bed, propped up the pillows of the bed against the headboard, and got back into bed in a sitting-up position to drink his coffee and to think about the day ahead. The day in question lay before him like a great uncharted ocean.

He wasn't thinking about last night. In fact, no images of the previous night were in his morning thoughts at all, but the fact was that he had been drinking at El Balcón the night before. El Balcón was a small bar in Villa Rosario, up on the second floor of a building, with a balcony that overlooked the Parque Central. Ricardo liked it because it was near his small apartment, and he would occasionally stop there on his way home from visiting the old man. He liked to sit with his drink on the balcony, look over the park at the taxi cabs lined up, the horse-drawn carriages, the young couples strolling arm in arm, and the prostitutes also strolling arm in arm as they trolled for clients. He sat there, drinking his drink, watching the scene in the park below him, and not thinking about anything in particular. But in the space of not thinking about anything in particular, Ricardo was no different than any other person, that is: his history, who he was, and all the paths that had led him to be where he was on this particular occasion were in the background of his mind, forming the context to what he was seeing. He wasn't thinking about anything in particular when he watched the horses pull the carriages along the dirt street, but he saw how skinny one particular horse was, and the context of his mind was that that his second wife, who had loved horses, would have been appalled at the treatment that these horses must receive working ten-to-fourteen hour days, wearing blinders, pulling the same wagon up and down the streets. He wasn't thinking about anything in particular when he watched the tops of the palm trees sway back and forth in the evening breeze, but the context of his mind signaled that there were no palm trees in the last city he had called home in the States. He wasn't thinking about anything in particular when his eyes followed any of the many women walking in the street below, but the context of his mind was that although he found some of them attractive and wanted to have sex with them, he was a gringo, and that presented certain barriers to any relationship. None of these thoughts were conscious to Ricardo. He was conscious only of the pleasant evening, of being slightly intoxicated and simply sitting on the balcony watching the world go by.

If he hadn't been thusly intoxicated, and so preoccupied with watching the people, and the horses, and the scenes in the park below his balcony viewpoint, he might have noticed that Magali had stepped into the bar. She was in the company of an older Panamanian man. And if Ricardo had seen them, he would not have known from first glance whether the man was a friend, a lover, or a sex client. But Ricardo did not see her, and thus was unaware that she and the man had entered the bar.

However, Magali saw Ricardo. She knew that Ricardo liked to occasionally go to El Balcón, and that there was a chance that Ricardo would be there that night, so when the man suggested they go there for a drink, she had hesitated before accepting the offer. As they entered the bar, Magali quickly scanned the inside, and when she saw Ricardo's silhouette sitting on the balcony, his back towards her, she turned to the man and quietly said, "I do not like it here. Let's go somewhere else," and then turned and walked out the door before the man could even answer. The man, of course, followed her out the door, and they did in fact go somewhere else.

But, as said, Ricardo was unaware of this event, and unaware that the sight of him had brought about a certain sadness in Magali. Ricardo simply continued sipping his drink, watching the world below, and letting his thoughts drift by.

And in the same way, this morning of the day in question, as he sat propped up in bed, sipping his coffee, thinking about the day ahead, he wasn't aware of the memory of sitting in the bar the night before. Although it, like everything else he had ever experienced, formed a context by which he viewed and understood his thoughts, Ricardo was only aware of his thoughts that morning, as he tried to plan his day. "I will have a piece of toast," he thought, "and some fruit, and then I will take a little jog before it gets too hot. Then after I return and shower, I'll make some breakfast. Then, I will write." He could not think of any errands he had to run today. He thought that he would write for a few hours, and then maybe call Miguel and see if he wanted to meet at the bathhouse in the afternoon. Because he hadn't received Carolina's email yet, and was unaware of her troubles at work, he assumed that he would take the bus to La Chorrera and met Miguel, that he would buy a bottle of Sangria later when he returned to Villa Rosario, and then that evening after dinner, he would stop by to see the old man, and that that would be his day.

And in fact, the first few steps of his plan, like the first steps of most plans, actually happened as planned. After he finished his coffee, he got up from the bed, pulled on a pair of running shorts and a t-shirt, and made some toast and cut up a small apple, and ate them. Then he put on his running shoes, stepped outside, locked his door, and started his customary run.

Villa Rosario was a small town, and while Ricardo lived only a few blocks from the center of town with its Parque Central and large Catholic Church, he also lived only a few blocks from the edge of town, with its cow pastures, dirt roads, small farms, and wooded areas. Ricardo had worked out his running route more than a year ago. It was a somewhat disjointed route, but it avoided the hilly streets, kept him on flat roads, took him past picturesque pastures, and avoided the streets that seemed to have the most loose dogs. Dogs were a problem in Villa Rosario, as they were in many Panamanian towns. Everyone seemed to keep one or two, for they served as early warning for intruders, burglars, and petty thieves. Thus, they were trained to bark at any stranger. And because they were never tethered, but stayed in the street outside of their respective homes, guarding their territory, there was nothing to prevent one from taking a nip at an unprotected ankle of a jogger running by. Jogging was a gringo hobby. Panamanians simply didn't do it. Ricardo had gotten over feeling conspicuous about it many years ago, but he was still wary of the dogs. Rabies was not uncommon in Panama, and any dog bite would require a trip to a hospital, and very likely a series of rabies shots.

But the jogging route that Ricardo had mapped out a year earlier was pleasant, free of dogs, and took him by places he liked to see. There was the town cemetery, with its hundreds of above-ground white concrete family mausoleums, each inscribed with the words "Familia de _____" with the family name at the end. Families would have purchased such mausoleums decades earlier, knowing that eventually, they would be used. A simple mausoleum would have four chambers, like horizontal slots, to hold four coffins, two on the bottom and two on top. When someone in the family died, their coffin would be slid into the empty chamber, and then the opening would be cemented over. Once the concrete cured, it would be painted white, to match the color of not only that mausoleum, but of all the mausoleums in the cemetery. Then a plaque with the deceased's name would be attached over the concrete seal. But until the chamber was filled with a coffin, it remained open, a gaping mouth into which the dead would eventually be fed. It must be strange, Ricardo had once thought, to look at your family's mausoleum, and see the empty slot where you knew that one day you would be buried. But that's how death was in Central America: a simple eventuality. People aged fast down here and died young.

The old man had told him once, "You gringos are such pussies about death. No one wants to die—it's horrible and painful and degrading—but you gringos never want to think about it. Here, it's always in our face. We make little candy skulls to give to the children. We have picnics in the cemetery. We sit with our family members when they die. Even the children sit. By the time a Panamanian reaches adulthood, he or she has seen four or five family members die."

But unbeknownst to the old man, Ricardo had seen death. While the old man was talking, Ricardo was remembering the first body he ever saw. The woman was lying on the examining table and the doctor was saying to Ricardo, "The bullet entered here," and he pointed to a small hole in her head, "and exited here," and he pointed to another larger hole on the other side of her head. Later, outside the examining room, Ricardo was talking to the cop who had brought the body in, and the cop was saying, "There was blood all over the wall and ceiling. That's how most suicides are. People think you die right away. You don't. You flip-flop on the floor like a fish in the bottom of a boat for about twenty minutes or so, spewing blood everywhere."

Ricardo gave his head a tiny twitch, as if to shake these images away. He had been sixteen at the time, doing volunteer work at the hospital. Yes, it was decades and decades ago, but the image was still clear and even after all that time. Ricardo didn't care to revisit the scene. The old man was still going on about how Panamanians were accustomed to death. Ricardo decided to divert the topic.

"Maybe you have to do that down here," Ricardo had replied. "The way everyone drives here, no one is safe. I take my life in my hands just crossing the street."

"Ha! That is true," said the old man, "but that's not

what I'm talking about. I'm talking about the fact that you gringos don't want to face the fact that you will die. You pay it lip service, but we kiss death on the lips. There is a difference."

"Yeah..." Ricardo said and then added quietly, "Well, I know I don't want to die."

"It comes sooner than you think," said the old man. "Sooner than anyone thinks."

* * *

Ricardo ran past the cemetery almost every morning, as he did on the morning of the day in question. Then his route took him down a wide dirt road lined with trees that overlooked a cow pasture. In the distance were mountains. There were rarely any people on this dirt road, and Ricardo found it peaceful to jog here. Then he ran down some streets past a factory that sold concrete building blocks for homes, and then finally up his street and back into his apartment.

There he showered and changed into a pair of shorts and a sleeveless t-shirt. Later, when he was to ride the bus to La Chorrera, he would change again into long pants and a shirt with sleeves and a collar. Except for wearing his jogging shorts when he ran, he never wore shorts in public. None of the Panamanian men did either. It was unseemly, no matter how hot or humid it was. But inside his apartment, of course, shorts and t-shirts were fine and helped keep him cool as each day heated up.

There was still plenty of coffee in the pot, and Ricardo poured himself a cup, added sweetener, sat down at his writing desk, opened his laptop and prepared to write.

The fact was, Ricardo spent most of his days writing. He had quit his job as a probate lawyer in that small town in New York years ago to move to Panama, so that he could devote himself to writing. He had sold a few short stories before he quit and had made one book deal, and those events gave him enough courage to quit his job. That, plus the fact that he had carefully analyzed his small savings and what his

Social Security payments would be if he took Social Security early—which he did decide to do—and he had concluded that he could survive in Panama with its lower cost of living until he could make a living off his books. However, that was many years ago, and while he had published several books since then—novels, short stories, and poems—he wasn't exactly making a living at it. The royalties dribbled in, and Ricardo continued to live off of his Social Security payments. Still, he never regretted his decision, because he enjoyed writing, and because the hope of eventually writing a best seller kept him going, as it does with thousands and thousands and thousands of other writers.

"Hope is a curse," the old man had once told him.

"Yeah, yeah, I know," said Ricardo. "Pandora's box and all that."

"No! I mean it's a curse in the full sense of the word," the old man continued. "In order to have a curse, you have to offend a god... and in order to offend a god, you have to be doing something you want in defiance of the arbitrary orders of the god, usually in defiance of the status quo. Some curses have time limits or antidotes. But hope is definitely one of the worst curses, because if you somehow get what you hope for, well, it's not always what's good for you. Sometimes it's the worst thing for you."

"Yeah," Ricardo said, "I think I follow you."

The old man leaned forward and lowered his voice. "You know, don Ricardo, I used to hope and pray that The Giant Fly would go away. It was so annoying to have him always in my way, no matter what I was doing, always going on and on giving me advice, but eventually I realized that I would miss him. I've grown to like him. So I'm glad I didn't get what I hoped for."

"Uh, that's a little different," Ricardo said.

"That's exactly what The Giant Fly always says! He says I'm a little different," the old man exclaimed.

"Well, he's right about that," said Ricardo.

This morning, on the day in question, Ricardo was working on a short story. He wasn't thinking about hope.

Rather, he was trying to craft a description of a particular character, a tattooed biker who was sitting in a low-lit dive bar. Ricardo was trying to use the minimal amount of words to describe how ominous the man was. He had decided on the biker's name "Road Rash" and that he worked as a debt collector for the motorcycle gang, and that this particular gang was in a state deep in the Midwest that didn't allow tattoos, so the gang made money by doing illegal tattooing. The gang made more money selling drugs and controlling hookers, but the tattoo business was a steady income stream and brought in new clients for the gang's other services. Most of their customers were young wannabe thugs or rebel girls, most of whom didn't have much money, but the gang sold them tattoos on the installment plan. You got your tattoo and paid twenty dollars a week or so until the debt was paid off. Road Rash was sitting in the bar explaining to a new client how the payment plan worked. The new client was a confused runaway girl of about seventeen, who was desperate to belong to any group that would befriend her. Road Rash was explaining that his job was to repossess the tattoo if the client didn't make the payments. "How do you repossess a tattoo?" the girl asked. Road Rash just pulled out a large knife from the sheath on his belt, and simply said, "I just cut them out."

Ricardo had been working on the story for about two hours, piecing together the words one by one, building the image of the bar, the large tattooed Road Rash sitting there, and describing how the girl had ended up there, when his laptop gave that beeping sound that indicated there was a new email.

Most of the emails that Ricardo received, like most of the emails that most people receive, were junk, but the banner at the top of the page indicated that this email was from Carolina, so Ricardo saved the story he was working on, and switched over to his email account and opened her email and read it. She had written:

"Hey, good morning. I really wish you were here so we could talk. I need your advice. I'm afraid they're going to fire me at work, and I don't want to get fired again. But they want me to file this petition to remove this child from her family, and I don't want to do it. They want me to lie and say that the child is in danger. But I went out to the home, and interviewed the child and the child's mother, and while they're poor, there's no abuse, no danger. It's crazy."

Ricardo hit the Reply button and typed: "Why does DSHS want to take the child?"

Carolina wrote back: "They've gotten sued so many times for *not* taking kids away from abusive parents, that now they're trigger happy. Their new policy is to remove a child if there's a complaint of abuse, even if the subsequent investigation can't substantiate the complaint. They're just doing it to cover their asses, but it's wrong. They've filed more petitions in the past two months than they filed all last year."

"Aren't you the social worker?" Ricardo wrote back. "Isn't the whole point of your job to determine if there's abuse?"

"Yes," Carolina replied, "but now they're overriding me. They're saying if I don't alter my findings and file a petition, they'll fire me."

"They can't do that!" Ricardo typed.

"Actually, I think they can. I've only been here five months. I'm still on probation. They can fire me for no reason at all. I'm going to try and make some calls during my lunch hour today, try and find a lawyer to see if I have any options. Maybe I can sue them, I don't know. But, I have to go to work now and can't talk, but can we Skype tonight? I'm desperate."

Ricardo replied immediately, "Of course. What time is good for you?"

And Carolina emailed back, "7:00? I'll be home by then."

Panama was on Eastern Standard time, the same time zone as Carolina was in. Ricardo wrote back, "That works for me. I'll make sure I'm here at my computer at 7:00 tonight."

"Thanks," came the short reply.

Ricardo sat at his desk and thought for a minute. A small knot had formed in his stomach. He hated it when people he cared about suffered. Even though he had no idea at this point what was going on with Carolina and her job, he knew she worked at DSHS and he knew she had integrity. So he felt confident that the problem lay with the people at DSHS. He had tried to dissuade her from taking the job when they offered it to her five months ago.

"You know, Carolina," he had said back then, "I've heard so many bad stories about that office. I mean, dealing with child abuse and child welfare cases is hard enough to start with. And I know it's been years since I lived there, but everything I heard when I did live there was that that office was full of fat tenured state workers who just don't give a shit. Are you sure you want to take this job?"

"I have no choice, Ricardo. I've been unemployed since I got fired four months ago. It's so hard to find a job in this field when you've been fired. It's like you get blacklisted. I need a job. DSHS doesn't pay much, but it's a job, and the health insurance is good."

"I understand, Carolina. Well, maybe you can keep looking while you're working there. Maybe there's a better gig somewhere."

"That would be nice."

So Carolina took the job and continued sending out resumes. But no other jobs materialized. As the week went by, she kept Ricardo posted on the politics in this DSHS field office where she was assigned—how the workers would wear their pajamas to work, and sit in cubicles and snack and gossip with each other all day. Ricardo kept advising her to keep a low profile and just try and do her job as best she could and to continue to send out resumes.

He remembered one of the old man's frequent rants about government agencies that try and help people. "They can't do it," the old man was saying. "No government agency can help people because they don't do it out of love. They may have a good idea, a great mission, but once they organize, and get managers, lazy selfish human nature kicks in, and their only mission becomes to protect their jobs and make the organization look good."

Ricardo rarely tried to challenge the old man when he was on his anti-bureaucracy rant, but one time he did.

"Love's got nothing to do with it," Ricardo told the old man. "The purpose of many agencies is simply to make sure the rules are followed."

"Love's got everything to do with it," the old man bellowed. "If you don't do something out of love, you never get off the wheel of life."

"Look," said Ricardo, "remember when you had that tooth removed at the dentist last month? I bet he had a tray of instruments on a small table by the chair where you were sitting, right? And those instruments are supposed to be sterilized, right? Whatever agency inspects dentists' offices down here doesn't need love to make sure that the dentist sterilizes those instruments. They just need to check his equipment and make sure he's following the proper sterilization method. You don't need love to check that."

"Ha!" the old man said. "We don't have dentist inspectors down here, señor gringo. We depend on the dentist to love us enough to sterilize his equipment."

"Jeez, there's no arguing with you sometimes," said Ricardo. "You always want to make every argument a solipsistic one."

"I don't even know what that word means," said the old man, "I'm just saying that if you don't do charity work with love, you don't find God. You know something that The Giant Fly told me once?"

"I can't wait to hear," said Ricardo.

"He told me that the first thing the Nazis did in Germany when they got into power was to create a Department of Relief. And they convinced the people that it would be more efficient to give money to one Department of Relief to do charity work instead of giving it to a thousand churches each doing a thousand programs. They said it would be more cost-efficient, that it would help more people, that it was more rational. And the people believed them, and stopped giving money to the churches and stopped doing volunteer work at the churches, and stopped helping the poor directly because there was a government agency doing it for them.

And you know the problem with that?"

"What?" asked Ricardo.

"It removed responsibility from the individual. They no longer had to care for the poor. They no longer had to care about anyone. They no longer had to love. Do you know where our Spanish word 'caridad' and your English word 'charity' comes from? They come from the Greek work 'caritas', which means 'love'. But it means individual love, not organizational love. This is why I am always suspicious when I hear about agencies doing charity. I think it's bullshit, like Nazi Germany."

"You know, there's not much arguing with The Giant Fly," said Ricardo.

Chapter 7: The Essence of Things

Ricardo thought about all these things as he sat at his desk after Carolina's emails on the morning of the day in question. He felt worried about her, and hoped that the Skype session that he had just agreed to have with her later that evening would answer some of his questions. He thought again about what it was like to be as young as she was, and to be trying to find a way through life while struggling to find a job or a career.

He got up from his writing desk, went into his kitchen and poured himself another cup of coffee. He felt the pot. It was cold. His coffee pot had one of those automatic switches that turned itself off after two hours, and it had been several hours since he had made coffee, sat in bed drinking it, gotten up, ran, showered, and spent time at his desk working on the story about Road Rash the tattoo repo man. He wondered if he should make another pot of coffee. He remembered that he had thought earlier that morning of calling Miguel and seeing if he wanted to go to the bathhouse that afternoon. He checked the clock on the stove—still a bit early to call Miguel. Miguel's job managing the restaurant that he co-owned with his wife's brother kept him up late at night. Plus, Ricardo realized that he hadn't made his own breakfast yet. He had not been hungry right after his run, and had gotten so engrossed in his writing that he had forgotten about his stomach. So, after realizing he needed to cook breakfast—now brunch—he decided, yes, he would make another pot of coffee. He poured the cold coffee from the pot into the sink, and put a new filter in the coffee maker and filled it with fresh coffee grounds. Images of Carolina kept appearing in his head as he poured water into the coffee maker. He couldn't stop thinking about how difficult it was to be young and idealistic in this world. It was hard enough when he was young, he thought, but today with all its internet and electronic distractions, it was almost impossible to keep sight of what was truly important, what was really meaningful.

As the coffee pot hissed and poured hot water through the coffee grounds into the pot, Ricardo remembered a conversation he had once had with the old man. The discussion—or maybe it would be more appropriate to call it a lecture—occurred when the old man had asked to borrow a CD player from Ricardo one night months ago during one of their nightly Sangria drinking sessions.

"Can you loan me your CD player?" the old man had asked.

"I don't have a CD player."

"Why not? How do you play your music?"

"I just listen to the radio or find music on the internet," Ricardo said. "I used to have a CD player, but I got rid of it, along with everything else, when I left New York and moved down here."

"Why did you get rid of it?" the old man asked.

"Well, I just wanted to simplify my life, to get down to the essence of things, you know. I didn't need it, or all my CDs, or most of the stuff I had."

"The essence of things?" the old man snorted. "I'll tell you what the essence of things is: It's sex and gold."

"Well, I don't know about that...." Ricardo started to say, but the old man interrupted him.

"Well, it's certainly not starvation and abstinence!"

"True," Ricardo laughed. "But what I meant was that I wanted to get rid of all the distractions in my life, and so many of my possessions felt like distractions."

"Ha," said the old man, "that's because you are a gringo. Only gringos feel the need to find themselves by giving away their possessions. No one does that down here. We find a use for everything."

"True," Ricardo said. "Would you like a refill?"

"Gracias, señor," said the old man. "But let me ask you this, don Ricardo, since you brought it up. What do you consider the essence of life to be?"

58

Ricardo refilled the old man's glass with Sangria. "Well," he said, "I don't think it is a thing; it's certainly not a thing you can get to... I think it's a process... that is, that the process of trying to get to the essence of things is in fact itself the essence of things, if that makes any sense."

The old man squinted and looked at Ricardo, and then he smiled. "And what about sex and gold?" he asked.

"Lots of rich people kill themselves, so gold can't be answer. But sex is closer to what I'm saying..."

"Yes!" shouted the old man. "I see what you mean. It's not cumming but getting to the orgasm that is the essence of sex."

"Yeah, well kinda, I guess," said Ricardo. "But what I'm trying to say is that I think that the struggle to get to a place, well not a place, but a lifestyle, a way of living, that only involves essential things, where you can be your authentic self and not be playing a role and just consuming more and more things, that it's *the process* that is essential."

The old man shook his head no in a disapproving way and said, "Does your *lifestyle*, as you call it, include sex?"

"Well, yeah... I guess it has to," Ricardo said. "Sex seems pretty essential."

"And how then, señor Ricardo, do you pay for your sex?" the old man asked in a taunting tone.

"Yeah, yeah, I know," Ricardo said. "Sex and gold. That's your answer to everything."

"No," said the old man, "it's not my answer to everything. But if you're going to be so stupid to talk about the *essence of things*, as if that solved any of life's problems, then I can talk about sex and gold as if they were answers."

The old man looked at Ricardo for a moment, then said, "I will tell you, don Ricardo, because I like you, and because you bring me wine, I will tell you a secret. The Giant Fly told me, so now I will tell you. There is no essence of things beyond what you have right now. That's the great irony of life. People spend their entire lives trying to get to nirvana, to some bullshit level of consciousness, only to find that it's the exact same level of consciousness they've had all along."

"Well, I don't know," said Ricardo. "I think that search for a higher level of consciousness is an attempt to better oneself... to improve one's self."

The old man laughed. "Can't be done! That's part of the great irony. No one is any more disciplined or smart or enlightened than they are right now, no more enlightened as they've always been."

"Oh, I don't believe that," Ricardo argued. "I'm happier down here than I was in the States. I think I'm a better person down here. My life is simpler. I feel like I'm living a more authentic life."

"Really?" said the old man. "A more authentic life? Really? Says the gringo who spends his money on prostitutes and gay bathhouses."

Ricardo laughed. "Touché, señor."

"What does that mean?" asked the old man.

"Oh, it's a French word that means, you make a good point," explained Ricardo.

"Flattery will get you nowhere," said the old man. "But you mentioned authenticity, and I think that's different. You do know, don't you, that it's impossible to be authentic when you're with other people." The old man smiled, looked at Ricardo, and waited.

"What do you mean?" asked Ricardo.

"Well, we're trained our entire lives to be a certain way around people, to be polite and courteous, or in some cases to be rebellious and obnoxious, but it's all habit, ingrained habit that kicks in as soon as we interact with another person. We have no choice. We are never authentic when we are with others. We're only authentic when we're alone... which, by the way, is why most people can't stand being alone. Whenever we are with other people, we are always playing a role."

"Ah, yes," said Ricardo. "All the world's a stage and all the men and women merely players, and one man in his time plays many parts..."

"That's good," said the old man. "You should put that in one of your books."

"I wish," said Ricardo, "but someone beat me to it."

*   *   *

Ricardo poured hot new coffee into his cup, remembering that conversation with the old man about the essence of things. He opened the refrigerator, removed eggs, butter, and a loaf of bread, and started making his late morning breakfast. And as he made his breakfast... and as he ate his breakfast... in fact, as he moved through the rest of day in question, doing things, going places, he was aware of a level of disquiet in his brain, a low-level hum of unease that would disappear when he was engaged in conversation or a specific activity, but would slowly creep back into his consciousness when there was a pause in whatever he was focusing on in that moment. If he had looked closely at this level of disquiet, he would have understood that the disquiet was his mind continuing to obsess about the essence of things, about the nature of change, about life itself, all prompted by the challenges that the old man had been making recently, the general concern that Ricardo had about his life choices, and the specific anxiety that Carolina's emails had sparked in him.

The general concern that Ricardo had about his life's choices was the general concern that all men, and all women, have in their lives, that point that everyone comes to somewhere between age forty and seventy, which is the question: *Is this all there is?* Before age forty, the question is easily discarded, because there is always the feeling of vast amounts of time ahead, so that if one feels unfulfilled in life, one simply tells oneself to work harder or be more patient—that the best is yet to come. But as the years tick slowly away, that answer is insufficient, and one must employ various skills to deal with the question. And Ricardo was as skilled as every man in keeping that question at arm's length, out of consciousness, pushed down and avoided. The problem was, the old man kept bringing it up, sometimes subtly and other times directly.

One time recently, for example, the old man just came out and asked him, "So... how are your books selling?"

"Eh... they're doing okay," Ricardo replied. "I'm not in the cut-out bins yet."

"I haven't seen your name on the New York Times best seller list," the old man said as he took a sip of Sangria.

"No," said Ricardo, "I haven't either."

"Do you feel like you made the right decision in moving here to Panama to write?"

Ricardo looked at the old man. He wasn't sure why this subject had come up, but the old man's face didn't have the usual mischievous look it had when he was teasing Ricardo. He looked serious.

"Well," Ricardo began, "I didn't really have a choice..."

"What?" the old man interrupted, "You, the big proponent of free will? Not have a choice? How could that be?"

"It's just an expression," Ricardo explained, feeling a bit annoyed. "Of course I had a choice. I could have stayed in Hamburg, New York, but there was nothing for me there. The winters are cold, the summers hot, and life is expensive. Panama was cheaper. I could not have afforded to retire and write if I had stayed in Hamburg. I would have been broke."

"You're broke here," the old man said dryly.

"*Not as broke...* or rather, I'm only broke here. I would have been bankrupt in Hamburg."

"Uh huh," the old man said, scratching his chin. "And what about your family and friends there? You left them all behind?"

"Well, to tell you the truth, there weren't any. I had no one up there."

"Really?" the old man asked in feigned surprise. "I seem to recall that you had several balls in the air at once, so to speak."

"None of them worked out."

"But I bet, señor Ricardo, that it is exactly the same down here, is it not?"

"What do you mean?"

"Well, refill my glass and I will tell you," the old man said as he extended his glass to Ricardo. Ricardo refilled it. The old man took a sip and started. "When you lived in New

York, you had the whores, right?"

"I don't like that word, but yes, there were the brothels in Canada, just over the border."

"And you had the bathhouses, right?"

"Yes... well, there were no bathhouses in Hamburg, but there were some nice ones in the nearby city of Buffalo, so yes."

"Okay, and you have Jenny's brothel down here, and the bathhouses down here, correct?"

"Yes."

"So, those things are exactly the same, whores and bathhouses. And you say that up there you had no one, yet you had several relationships that fell apart, right?"

"Uh huh..."

"And down here you had that alley cat and that sweet whore at Jenny's, what was her name?"

"Magali... and where is this conversation going?" Ricardo asked.

"It's going to my point that your life is exactly the same down here as it was in the States. Nothing is any different. And do you know why that is, don Ricardo?"

"I can't wait."

"It's because people can't change. Why would your life be any different down here than it was up there? You're the same person... thus, you're going to create the same problems for yourself down here as you had up there."

Ricardo was feeling defensive. He hated it when the old man got on his confrontation kick.

"The difference is, I can write down here!"

"You wrote up there. Didn't you tell me that you only quit your job *after* your first book was published?"

"Right, but it took me three years to write that book, because I had to work to make a living! Since I moved down here, I've published eight other books!" Ricardo was almost shouting now.

"I still don't see your name on the New York Times list of best sellers," said the old man.

"And your point?" asked Ricardo angrily.

"My point, don Ricardo, is that if you quit your job

and moved down here to write... If all your effort and travel was to get to this place to do this thing... why aren't you better at it? Hmmmm?"

Ricardo opened his mouth to reply, but then shut it and was silent. He felt a burning behind his eyes, but knew that the old man had not said anything that he himself had not felt.

Finally Ricardo said, "I don't have an answer to that, señor. I like what I write. I enjoy writing. It... it fills my day, and somehow gives my life meaning. I never planned on making a fortune off of it. In fact, I only made the move down here once I determined that I could live just on my Social Security alone. The fact that I sell a few hundred books a month gives me great pride, but it may be that's all I'll ever sell. And at that rate, I don't think you'll ever see my name on any best seller list. But... it's what I do. My fate, I guess."

"Fate..." mused the old man. "Yes, I think it is your fate... Interesting word, fate... don't you think, don Ricardo? The place where all of one's personal choices lead, almost as if the choices didn't make... any... difference... at... all..." The old man's voice trailed off, but he was smiling, as if remembering a private joke.

*   *   *

Had Ricardo looked closer at the level of disquiet he was experiencing as he moved through the day in question, he would have been aware that his mind was replaying that confrontation over and over again. But of course, Ricardo was not aware that he was processing it. That's how the mind works: everything is being processed, analyzed, discussed, dissected, reformulated and replayed just below the line of our awareness, bubbling there just below the thousand and one things we do to occupy our time. At times it seems we do everything and anything to distract ourselves from simply being aware of what we are actually thinking about at that moment. And what Ricardo was actually thinking about, actually processing on the day in question, just like everyone else in this wide world, is how utterly meaningless and barren his own life was. But of course, that's how life is. The utter meaninglessness of it always lurks just beyond our consciousness, like that dream we just can't seem to remember. And so it was with Ricardo, as he moved through the day in question. However, on the day in question, the disquiet he was experiencing was humming louder than usual, because Carolina's emails had stirred him up. Something about them, about her, about her situation, disturbed him, resonated with him, resonated and amplified that usual question in his general background of disquiet, that question of what difference does personal choice make in a life that is so empty. And as he moved through his day, his mind continued to churn through his memories: his memory of Carolina, his awareness of her choices, his questions about his own choices in life, his feelings towards her, his feelings towards other women he had known, the times when he had actually felt love and connection, and the more numerous times he had felt disconnected from anyone and anything. As indicated, Ricardo was unaware of the specific reflections and recollections that his mind was dealing with—he was only dimly aware of the feeling of disquiet being a bit more intense on this day in question. But all the while, all day long, his mind was busy replaying every single conversation he had ever had with Carolina, and every single conversation he had ever had with the old man, all replaying simultaneously with every memory he ever had of love, and every thought he ever had about his work, about the life he had, and about the life he had left behind.

Chapter 8: Magali

Despite the fact that Ricardo had not seen Magali walk into El Balcón the night before, for some reason an image of her popped into his mind on the day in question. It was after his late breakfast, and after the time he had called Miguel and arranged to meet him in the center of La Chorrera at the bathhouse. Ricardo had caught the late morning bus to La Chorrera, and because it was late morning, the bus was not crowded and he had found a seat. Many thoughts ran through his head as the bus traveled the thirty-minute direct route to La Chorrera, the same route that Ricardo would ride in reverse later that afternoon, but at some point that morning on that bus, the image of Magali rose up in his consciousness.

Perhaps it was, as discussed, the fact that his subconscious was unusually active that day, churning over details and memories of his life, a life that included a brief love affair with Magali; or perhaps it simply was that memories of her often crossed his mind; or perhaps, as the metaphysicians would have us believe, the proximity and vibration of her the night before—standing in the entranceway to El Balcón, some seventy feet away from where Ricardo was sitting—was enough for his skin to sense her presence and convey that impression to his mind. Or maybe there was the more scientific explanation: that a few hundred molecules of her perfume had wafted their way across the room the night before, mixing with the thousands of other smells in the bar that night, and had buried their scent deep into his subconscious... But for whatever reason, the image of her rose up from the depths that day as he was riding the bus, staring out of the window—rose up to the point that he became aware that he was remembering her.

He had met her several years ago, under circumstances

that do not concern us here save for the place of his meeting: Jenny's brothel. Jenny had selected Magali for Ricardo because, unlike most of Jenny's patrons, Ricardo liked his women slim and small-chested. Magali was that: slim, dark-skinned, with black hair cut short. Ricardo had started off as her customer, but soon was dating her outside of the brothel, and for a brief while, they even lived together at Ricardo's small apartment in Villa Rosario, until Ricardo ended the affair one day because of her previously described requests for money.

But the image that rose up to Ricardo's mind on this day was a pleasing one: bittersweet, in that they were no longer lovers, but pleasing to remember. The image was of her standing there naked, having just come out of the bathroom, about to walk over to the bed where she and Ricardo had been lying. There was a small white towel in her hand, and in his mind's eye, he watched her dry her hands with the towel, look over at him and smile, toss the towel over the back of a chair, and climb back into bed with him. Her dark skin was unblemished, smooth and shiny. Ricardo watched her small breasts with their almost-black nipples sway as she bent down towards the bed and placed her hands on the bed to climb in. As she lifted one knee up onto the bed, his eyes lingered over the mass of dark curly public hair that exploded up from underneath and behind her pussy up over her crotch and up her abdomen almost to her waist. Ricardo loved to bury his head in that grove of hair, letting it caress his face as he found and licked her pussy, running his tongue up and down both sides of those dark pussy lips, finding the clit, licking it, sucking it, then thrusting his tongue into her vagina, tasting the juices, and sliding up to nibble at her clit again, all the while grasping both legs under the knee joints with his hands and pushing them up and apart with his arms. She would moan, and push back with the strength of both her legs until eventually his arms gave way, and her dark legs fell over his shoulders, over his back, while his hands reached up to fondle her breasts as he continued to lick and suck, manipulate and thrust into her pussy.

The first time he had tried to go down on her, she was surprised, even a little scared. It is not a Panamanian practice, and she had not experienced it with many men before Ricardo. Nor was it a practice that Ricardo would have performed on other women of Magali's profession. But Ricardo knew that Jenny was extremely conscientious—almost obsessive—about regularly testing her girls for STDs. He knew this because he had become friends with Jenny over the years. It was a friendship that didn't allow for any discounts, because Jenny was all business; but it was a friendship nonetheless, and they had often talked about her business. Jenny ran a tight house, had a rigorous testing schedule for her girls, and always required that they use condoms.

None of these particular details were part of the memory that rose up in Ricardo's mind this particular morning, however. There was only the image of Magali coming out of the bathroom naked, drying her hands and tossing the small white towel over the back of the chair, and climbing back into bed. Just that single image, like a short video that replayed about five or six times in Ricardo's mind, and then wistfully sank back down as something outside the bus window caught his eye, and his mind drifted onto other thoughts, which is the way that mind and memory and consciousness work.

The subject of memory and consciousness was one of the old man's constant topics. Ricardo often had wondered why the old man was so obsessed with them, but the fact was, the old man usually became obsessed with anything he developed an interest in.

"Do you realize," the old man lectured Ricardo one day months ago, "that every second of our lives we are floating on a sea of memory? It's a sea that is infinitely deep, full of beautiful fish, mermaids, sunken ships loaded with treasure, mysterious coral reefs, and tons of plastic trash, pollution and other flotsam. And while we are only concerned with the single wave that is holding afloat at that moment, the fact is we are surrounded by an infinite number of waves each full of thousands of memories, all of it at our fingertips... Do you realize how fantastic it is, don Ricardo?"

"Yeah, I guess," said Ricardo.

"Well, of course you don't," the old man laughed. "How could you? You're like all of us, clutching to our little rafts, trying to stay afloat, hoping we don't drown, concerned only with the immediate shark-infested waters around us." The old man broke into a fit of laughter, and then said, "Well, thank God, there is Sangria on our little rafts, eh don Ricardo?"

It was true—the old man loved his Sangria. Ricardo had discovered that two years before the day in question, back when he had first met the old man in the Parque Central of Villa Rosario. The old man was sitting on one of the concrete benches that line the park, and seemed rather ill. Ricardo had noticed him try to stand up, unsuccessfully, and then sit back down. Ricardo had walked up to him and asked if he was alright, and if he needed any help. The old man had explained that it was his first day out of his apartment in a week; that he had just gotten over the flu; but that he had obviously bit off more than he could chew in walking from his apartment down to the park; and he felt exhausted.

While the old man was explaining all this to Ricardo in the park, Ricardo was accessing him. The old man was indeed old, but didn't look feeble. He just seemed exhausted by his exertion. Also, Ricardo noticed that he didn't smell like an old man. Many of the geriatrics who hung around the park obviously neglected their personal hygiene, but this old man didn't. His small beard was neatly trimmed, his hair brushed, and his clothes, while not new, were clean. Because of these observations, and because the old man's story seemed true, Ricardo decided to help him. Ricardo asked him where he lived, and the old man told him. It was about a ten minute walk from the park, but probably ten minutes more than the old man needed.

"Let me help you back to your apartment," Ricardo said. "Come on, I'll get a taxi."

"Oh señor, I do not have money for a taxi," the old man said.

"That's okay, señor, I will pay for it," Ricardo said, and

helped the old man stand up.

They walked to the corner of the park, where a line of taxis always waited, and selected one. Ricardo helped the old man into the back seat and then sat down next to him. The old man gave the driver the address, but then added that he needed to make one quick stop at the local supermercado on his way home.

"It will just take a minute," the old man assured Ricardo. Ricardo assumed that he needed to buy one or two items of food, and so he agreed. But when the taxi stopped in front of the supermercado, the old man handed Ricardo approximately four dollars in Panamanian balboas and asked, "Would you be so kind, señor, to run inside and buy me a bottle of Sangria?" And he named the brand.

Ricardo was taken back, but having gone this far in offering the old man the ride home, he complied with the request. He went inside, made the purchase, and returned to the taxi.

"It was the reason I ventured out today," the old man explained as they rode towards the old man's apartment. "I was too sick to go out the past few days, and I had to do without the water of life... but I thought I had recovered enough to make the trip today."

Ricardo listened without responding, but then the old man launched into a lengthy explanation of how Sangria is made, its origins in Spain and Portugal, the correct recipe for brewing it, why honey is the preferred sweetener rather than sugars, and a comparison of whether red wine, white wine or mulled wine is the proper base for making Sangria. Ricardo was impressed by the old man's depth of knowledge on the subject, impressed enough that he returned to the old man's apartment a few days later, ostensibly to check on him, But he brought him another bottle of Sangria and spent the next two hours listening to the old man pontificate on Sangria, the time-space continuum, the politics of the Basque movement in Spain, the history of the woman's movement in Panama, and the general decline in human intelligence all over the world. That was the start of Ricardo's frequent visits to the old man, visits that always included

Ricardo providing the Sangria.

Over time, the visits became part of Ricardo's daily schedule, simply something he automatically did every evening. If he knew he was going to be out of town on a particular evening, he would bring the old man an extra bottle of Sangria on the visit beforehand, as if to apologize for his upcoming absence. The old man was always there inside his little apartment, no matter what time of evening Ricardo arrived. Ricardo would walk the ten minutes from the center of town to the old man's apartment, up the stone stairs to knock at the apartment door. The old man would shout at him from within to enter. Ricardo would present him with the bottle of Sangria each time as if it was the first time he had ever brought him a bottle. The old man would thank him graciously and invite him to sit. And they would sit and chat... or rather, Ricardo would sit and listen, for one to two hours, while they both drank Sangria. When the bottle was finished, Ricardo would say his goodbyes. Ricardo was always conscientious about letting the old man drink most of the bottle, mostly because the old man enjoyed the wine, but also because Ricardo knew that El Balcón lay on his walking route back to town, and Ricardo could—and often would—stop there on the walk back for a nightcap or two, or three.

There were times when the old man's weird stories, twists of logic, and crazy opinions exasperated Ricardo, but most of the time Ricardo was enthralled by the old man's stories, which is why he returned night after night. It was as if the old man would grab a random topic like a slippery moray eel and Ricardo would watch the topic twist and turn in the old man's hands. Sometimes the eel would turn and bite Ricardo when Ricardo least expected it.

"Did I ever tell you that I met your famous Sigmund Freud one time?" the old man suddenly asked Ricardo during one visit.

"Really?" Ricardo said, while he tried to calculate the years in his head to see if that could actually be possible. "When was that?"

"I don't remember how long ago it was, don Ricardo,

but he was an old man then, and I was quite young, just a boy. He used to give lectures you know, all over the world. I think he did it for the money, to support his cocaine habit."

"Um... he stopped using cocaine when he was a young man," said Ricardo.

"Well, of course he would say that," the old man retorted. "But you can never trust a druggie, you know that. They'll say anything."

"Well, okay... where did you meet him?"

"It was in Panama City. My father took me to see him. He was giving a lecture at some university. He spoke in German but had a Spanish translator. My father was very impressed by him. As I say, I was only a boy, maybe seven or eight years old, but even then, I knew that he was full of shit."

"Really? Why did you think that?" Ricardo asked.

"Well, he was just so full of himself. I had read his books, and most of them were pretty good, except for his bullshit about dreams, but when he spoke, it was all *me me me*. *I* discovered this, and *I* discovered that, like he was the first guy in the world to realize that people were self-deluded lying little hypocrites."

"Wait a minute," said Ricardo, "you had read his books by age seven?"

"Yup."

"Umm, why?"

"Well, it was my mother's doing. She promised that she would buy me a rifle if I read at least two of his books. I really wanted that rifle, so I read them. The only one I really liked was *Civilization and Its Discontents*. He hit the name on the head in that one. But you know what the kicker was?"

"What?"

"I never got the rifle. My mother reneged on the deal. Said I was too young. So to console me, my father took me to see him speak. But it just added salt to the wound... he was such a crappy speaker, so full of himself. At the end of the lecture, I even raised my hand and asked him a question."

Ricardo shook his head and then asked, "Really? What did you ask him?"

"I asked him, after all his investigations into the human mind, what one thing did he conclude?... and do you know what the bastard answered?"

Ricardo took a big breath. "No, what did he say?"

"He said, and I quote, 'Life is just so confusing sometimes.' That was his big conclusion. My father was so proud of me for asking the big Sigmund Freud a question, but I thought the guy was an imbecile. Hell, I knew that life wasn't confusing and I was only seven years old. I was so mad I refused to talk to my father during the entire bus ride home."

Ricardo thought it best to not ask any more questions specifically about Sigmund Freud, so instead he asked, "So you don't think life is confusing?"

"No, of course not! Do you?"

"Yeah, yeah at times I do," Ricardo answered.

"Hmm... it's because you are a gringo," the old man announced. "Gringos are always confused. I think it must be part of your political system."

"Well, I can't argue with that," Ricardo said, glad to be off the topic of Freud. But then the old man asked, "And you know something else about the big Sigmund Freud?"

Ricardo   sighed,   "What?"

"He was afraid of doorways. It's true. He had a morbid fear of walking through doorways. The big Sigmund Freud, afraid of a doorway. Even I could psycho-analyze that one. Doorway, threshold, new beginnings. Tell me, don Ricardo, are you afraid of doorways?"

"Doorways? No, can't say that I am." Ricardo thought about it for a moment more and then added, "Although, there are some doors that when you walk through them, you can't turn back."

"Ah, yes," the old man said. "Commitment. I see where you are going with this, don Ricardo... the fear of commitment. Are you afraid of commitment, don Ricardo?"

"Sometimes, yeah, sure. Who isn't?"

"Like commitment to your alley cat? Didn't she want to get married and you said no? And then that door was closed to you?"

Ricardo tightened up a little. "Well, she never brought

it up directly... and I never did either... but I always felt that she did, and I didn't..."

"Do you know, don Ricardo, what Socrates said about marriage?"

"Uh... no."

"Well, young Euripides was engaged, and he asked Socrates if she should get married, and Socrates said, and I quote, 'By all means, marry. If you get a good wife, you'll be happy, and if you get a bad wife, you'll be a *philosopher*!'" The old man broke into a fit of laughter, and then said, "I always love that joke."

*   *   *

None of those many conversations with the old man rose into Ricardo's conscious mind on the bus ride to La Chorrera that late morning. The only things he was conscious of during that ride were the one image of Magali naked, the ever-changing view out the window of the bus and, of course, various images of the bathhouse where he was going to meet Miguel in a short while. The images of the many times he had been there before, images of the steam room, the whirlpool, the hallways, the various small rooms, and the many, many men who wandered through those darkened halls and rooms looking for... well, looking for the myriad of things that men look for in bathhouses.

Chapter 9: Time

As Ricardo was deep in his thoughts on the bus ride to La Chorrera, or to be more accurate, as Ricardo was simply floating on the sea of thought on his tiny raft of self-awareness, almost hypnotized by his lack of focus, he was completely unaware of time as the minutes slipped by. The bus ride took exactly thirty-three minutes, right on its usual schedule, and it was approaching the stop on the block of the bathhouse where Ricardo would exit the bus. The sight of the familiar buildings on that block jostled his little mental raft and he suddenly started to focus on getting himself ready to pull the cord and stand up and make his way off the bus. But up until that block, he was still in his hypnotic reverie and, as stated, completely oblivious to time.

"Time is the opposite of love," the old man had told him once. "Whereas love disappears the moment you look at it, time *only* appears when you look at it. You know why? It's because time doesn't exist unless you think about it."

Usually Ricardo just let the old man ramble when he got onto his metaphysical kick, but on this one, Ricardo argued back. "Just because you're not thinking about something doesn't mean it doesn't exist. Just because you're not thinking about what's in your refrigerator doesn't mean that the food there doesn't exist."

"Ha," the old man snickered. "My refrigerator is empty."

"Whatever," said Ricardo.

"No, seriously don Ricardo. Time is not what you think it is." The old man paused for a minute, and then said, "Did you know, don Ricardo, that you could bend light?"

"Well, you mean like in those fiber optic cables?"

"No, that's not bending; that's just the light bouncing

and reflecting off the insides of the cable. I mean actually bending light as it moves through space."

Ricardo thought about this for a moment, and then said, "No, no, I don't think you can. It has to reflect off something."

"No," said the old man. "Gravity can bend light. It's one of the phenomena that scientists study during eclipses, how the starlight from distant stars is bent as it passes by our sun, by the gravity of our sun."

"I didn't know that," Ricardo said, and thought about it for a minute. "I always thought light was like energy, like a wave, something without mass, but you're saying that it's affected by gravity?"

"Yup."

"Okay, señor, for the sake of argument, or in your case, for the sake of avoiding an argument, let's say that light can be bent. What about it?"

"Well," the old man said. "If gravity can bend light, why can't gravity bend time?"

"Because time is not a thing. It doesn't have mass."

"Neither does light," smiled the old man.

"Okay," said Ricardo. "Assuming waves or energy can be bent by gravity, time isn't either one of those, either."

"Yet, time slows down near a black hole..." Now the old man was grinning.

"Really?" asked Ricardo.

"Well, that's what your famous Einstein said. He also said that time slows down when you accelerate, and that the closer you get to the speed of light, the slower time moves."

"That explains why you look so young, señor," Ricardo said. "Okay... still, assuming that's true, so what? What is your point?"

"My point, don Ricardo, is that time is not what you think it is. Ever notice how when you're waiting for a lover to show up at your door, time drags on? But how when she is in your bed, there's never enough time, how it flies by?"

Ricardo laughed. "Of course. It's a universal complaint."

"And," the old man continued, "how when you're with

78

someone you don't like, how times seems to slow to a crawl?

"Like in-laws?" Ricardo quipped.

"Yes, exactly! Well, I've been thinking that there might be other forces that affect time rather than just gravity."

"Permit me to interrupt, señor," said Ricardo, "but aren't those just human perceptions of time? The things we desire consume us, so we perceive the time we have with them as shorter, and likewise we're counting the minutes until we can get away from the people we don't like. It's just our... our experience of these things, our perceptions of them... our consciousness of them."

"Ah, don Ricardo," said the old man. "Once again you have beaten me to the punch. That's exactly the point I was going to mention—our consciousness of things bends time."

"Is that in Einstein's theory?" Ricardo asked.

"No, but he was limited," the old man said. "He missed the obvious truths. In fact, The Giant Fly showed me where Einstein was totally wrong about some things. For example, do you know when time stops?"

Ricardo thought for a moment, and then quipped, "when you're dead?"

"Exactly!" the old man shouted. "And do you know why that is?"

Ricardo had not been serious when he answered with the "dead" comment, but he didn't tell the old man that. Rather, he said, "because you're not able to perceive time?"

"Exactly!" the old man said. "Without perception, or rather, without consciousness, there is no time."

"Well, what about when we're asleep?" Ricardo asked.

"What about it? When we're asleep we always experience time, one way or another. No, time stops when we're dead, and that's because it doesn't exist unless we're alive. Now here's the ironic thing... and I confess don Ricardo, I can't quite understand it myself. The Giant Fly has tried to explain it to me, but I can't, as you gringos say, get my head around it, so I will just tell you what he said. He said that time does not exist when you're dead, because you're no longer conscious, but that time also does not exist when you're totally conscious."

"Maybe he was speaking metaphorically," Ricardo suggested.

"Well, I asked him that, but he said no, that he was speaking specifically. He told me that a person could slow down time by being conscious of it."

Ricardo refilled the old man's glass with Sangria and topped his off as well. Then he said, "Well, señor, really, what does it all matter? Where does it get us? Whether time is real or not, we're stuck in the time we're stuck in, so what does it matter? It's just not relevant to my daily life."

"Well, don Ricardo, I will tell you the secret that The Giant Fly told me, which is why the whole subject became suddenly relevant to my life. Everybody knows that time is slower when you're a child, right? Summers seem to last forever. A year is an eternity, right?"

"Yeah, right... I mean, it seems that way when you're young," Ricardo replied.

"Not *seems*—it *is* that way!" the old man blurted. "The Giant Fly explained it to me. Those black holes are death! He said that Einstein got it totally backwards. Time actually that time speeds up as you approach a black hole. The black hole of our death is pulling us towards it, and the closer we get, the faster we go. Our life *is* accelerating as we get older— well, not as we get older but as we get closer to death, we're going faster and faster—time is actually speeding up for us. *That's* why we experience life as faster when we're older—it *is* faster. And that means the faster you feel your life going by, the closer you are to death. So if your life feels like it's going by too fast, it means you are very close to death."

Ricardo took a long sip of his Sangria and studied the old man. He had to be over eighty years old, Ricardo thought, maybe even close to ninety. Maybe it was natural— when you're that old—to think about death a lot. Still, the image of time accelerating towards death was intriguing.

"So you think death is literally the ultimate gravity?" Ricardo asked

"Yup," the old man said. "That what The Giant Fly calls it—the *black hole of death* is his phrase."

"Even if that's true, señor, we can't stop that. The time of our death is written, as they say."

"Ha, says the man who believes in free will!" the old man laughed. "But that's the point, don Ricardo... that's what The Giant Fly was trying to teach me. He told me that you can slow the process down by being conscious, that somehow just thinking about time can slow the acceleration down."

"Really? I thought a person was only as young as they feel, not as young as they think," joked Ricardo.

"No, seriously, don Ricardo, The Giant Fly said it was possible to slow the slide toward death down by concentrating on time. He gave me a riddle to think about, a riddle that he said would slow time down. Do you want to hear it?"

"Sure, why not?" said Ricardo.

"It's complicated," said the old man.

"Lay it on me," said Ricardo.

"Okay. The Giant Fly asked me what the name of a zero-dimensional object was, and I told him a 'point.'"

"Okay," agreed Ricardo.

"And then he asked me what was the name of the space between two zero-dimensional objects, and I said a 'line segment'. And he asked me to confirm that this was a one-dimensional object, that is, that a line segment only has one dimension: length. And I said yes. And then he asked me what the space between two line segments was, and I said a 'plane', and he asked me to agree that this was a two-dimensional object, having length and width, and I of course said yes. Then he asked me what was the name of the space between two of these two-dimensional objects, and I said a 'cube', and then I agreed with him that a cube was a three-dimensional object... and this is where he stuck me... he asked me what was the name of the space between two three-dimensional objects, and I didn't know what that was called. I told him it was 'space' but he said no; he said it was time—that *time* was the fourth dimension. But the only thing I could think of was the time it took you to get from one three-dimensional object, like a building,

81

to another building, but he said it was the relationship between the buildings. And he forced me to agree with him that this was the fourth dimension, which made sense, since the third dimension was the relationship between two two-dimensional objects, the fourth dimension had to be the relationship between two three-dimensional objects. And *then* he asked me what was the name of the space between two four-dimensional objects... and I was stymied. If time was the fourth dimension, then the fifth dimension could only be the relationship between two different times, and the sixth dimension could only be the relationship between two different time relationships and so on and so on to infinity. The Giant Fly told me that if you think about that riddle long enough, you could slow time down."

"Or drive yourself nuts," said Ricardo. "Do you often have these conversations with The Giant Fly?"

"Oh sí, don Ricardo, we talk every day."

*   *   *

Ricardo got off the bus in front of the bathhouse and looked at his watch. He was right on time. He walked about twenty feet from the bus stop to the unmarked door of the bathhouse and went inside.

Of course, at no point on this day, the day in question—and certainly not as he entered the bathhouse—did Ricardo know that in fact Carolina *was* going to be fired the next day. Despite her prepared letter of resignation that she would read to him later that night; despite her preparations; despite her semi-support from the Attorney General's office; despite her good work; despite her degree; despite her good initial work reviews; despite her good client rapport; despite all that, she would be called into the Director's office as soon as she arrived at the job the next morning, and told that her department was being "reorganized" and that unfortunately her services were no longer needed, and security would stand there while she cleaned out her office and escort her back to her car. Nor did Ricardo know that Carolina would call him the next day crying and tell him all this; nor would either one of them know the next day and in the days to come, that all her subsequent efforts to gain justice—all her written complaints with the Human Relations Commission, and all her subsequent conversations with attorneys—would all be to no avail. Time would pass and, as the old man had predicted, the DSHS office would continue to be operating the same way, and would be operating the same way for years to come. None of this knowledge was available to Ricardo on the day in question, and certainly not as he walked through the bathhouse door. Because he, like all of us, was stuck in time.

Besides, as he walked through the bathhouse door, he was focused on other, more immediate, matters. As indicated, his mind was focused on the things that men look for in bathhouses: sex, relief, contact, sanctuary, escape, numbness, flesh, and of course, love.

Chapter 10:   Love

Love was another topic on which the old man had many diverse and sometimes contradictory opinions.

"Do you remember what Jesus said about love?" the old man had asked Ricardo one evening recently.

"As I recall," Ricardo responded, "He said a lot of things about love. Which one are you referring to?"

"I'm referring to his comments on sexual love," the old man answered.

"Well, in that case, no, I don't remember that. I don't recall Jesus ever talking about sexual love."

"Well he did," the old man said. "Someone asked him if there was marriage in heaven, and he said 'no'... which is amazing, when you consider how much the church pushes marriage. Anyway, he said that there was no marriage in heaven but there was sexual love."

"Uh, I don't recall him saying it exactly that way," Ricardo said. "He didn't say 'sexual love'—he just said there was love in heaven."

"If you go back to the original Hebrew text, and the first Greek translations, it says 'sexual love'. It's only in the later Latin translations that those uptight monks changed the translation to just 'love'. Ironic really, when you think about it...those monks, living their pious lives in the monastery; 'heaven on earth' they used to call those places; with all their devout meditations; why, they were fucking each other every day, up and down the cloisters, so to speak. I think they changed the translation to cover up their own sexuality."

"No doubt," said Ricardo. "But how do you know that's what the original Hebrew words meant?"

"Trust me," said the old man, "I've researched this in depth. The original biblical writings have Jesus saying there was no marriage in heaven, but there was sexual love. That's where the Muslims get all that 'virgins in heaven' crap, as if fucking virgins was somehow better than fucking experienced women."

"You've lost me again," said Ricardo. "You started by asking me if I knew what Jesus said about love..."

"Oh, yes... thank you, don Ricardo. The Sangria sometimes lubricates my mind too much. My point was that Jesus was saying that the best part of love, the *only* part they allow in heaven, is the feeling of love, the expression of love, and specifically, the physical expression of love... but not the living together, not the bounds of matrimony, not the shackles of marriage."

"So, what are you saying? That heaven is just a bunch of angels fucking each other all day, changing partners endlessly?" Ricardo asked.

"Well, I'm just quoting Jesus, but basically, yes, that's what he said."

"Well, that's hardly a traditional Catholic view, señor," Ricardo said.

"I never said I was a traditional Catholic, don Ricardo. But I am not concerned with heaven. I think Jesus was just trying to make a point about what was important. You and I know, and even Jesus knew, that there is no heaven—it's just a way of talking about things."

"Uh huh," said Ricardo, "and what *are* we talking about here."

"I would have thought a man of your lack of moral code would be following me better," the old man chided. "What we are talking about is love. What do you think love is, don Ricardo?"

"Christ! Who knows?" Ricardo exclaimed.

"Exactly!" the old man exclaimed. "Once again, don Ricardo, you have tricked me and gone to the core of the issue. You are such an intelligent man! That's why I love conversing with you. That and, of course, the fine Sangria you so thoughtfully bring me. You don't know what love is, because no one knows what love is. No one knows! The original Greeks had to use six different Greek words to translate the word love from the Hebrew, and the original Hebrew had at least ten words for love."

"Really?" said Ricardo, "I didn't know that about the Hebrew text."

"It's true! And the telling thing is, that despite all ten of those Hebrew words, they weren't enough. Jesus and what-his-name, that goofball Paul who couldn't shut up about Jesus, they both had to keep trying to define it. 'Love is unselfish; love builds others up; love is not angry; love is this; love is that' et cetera. Did you know that there are two hundred forty-seven different attempts in the New Testament to define what love is?"

"Really?" said Ricardo. "Did you count them?"

"I didn't have to," exclaimed the old man, "The Giant Fly counted them for me. And do you know why they had to keep trying to define love in so many different ways?"

"No, tell me," Ricardo said.

That familiar mischievous smile crept across the old man's face. Then he said, "Maybe they couldn't define it because it doesn't exist, so they kept trying to figure out different ways of describing it, so they could continue to sell it. Maybe love doesn't exist at all."

Ricardo looked at him carefully. He wasn't sure exactly where this discussion was going, but that was usually the case with the old man. The old man continued to smile and extended his hand holding an empty glass to Ricardo. Ricardo filled his glass with Sangria, and then gently said, "I don't believe that."

"No one does," said the old man. "That's why we have love songs, and love movies, and love stories. Maybe love is kinda like God himself—God only exists because we need him to exist, and love only exists because we need it to exist."

"Well, señor," Ricardo started, "I've heard that argument before. It's the pessimist's argument. It's like saying people shouldn't get married because most marriages fail, but people still want to get married. Just because people can't seem to sustain love doesn't mean that love doesn't exist."

"Fine, then," the old man said. "Then you define it.

What is it?"

"I can't," admitted Ricardo. "I can't, because I don't know what it is... but that doesn't mean that it doesn't exist. I was married twice, and I loved both of those women. The fact that we failed to sustain a marriage, or that that any relationship ends in anger or bitterness, doesn't mean that you didn't love the person. Just because we are incapable of shouldering the responsibility of love doesn't mean that love doesn't exist."

"Responsibility of love?" scoffed the old man. "Do you think love is a job? That hardly sounds romantic. No, don Ricardo, I think you are confusing love with a relationship. One takes on the responsibility of a relationship; that is different. What I am talking about here is what Jesus was talking about: sexual love, that overwhelming desire to possess, devour, invade, penetrate or be penetrated by another person, to lose oneself in a complete physical union."

"Wait a minute!" exclaimed Ricardo. "I thought you just said love didn't exist."

"Did I? Oh no, you misunderstand. I was just saying that some people might argue that," said the old man.

"Jesus fucking Christ, you can be exasperating sometimes, señor," Ricardo said.

"Yeah, that's what The Giant Fly tells me sometimes, too," said the old man. "No... if I implied that I believe that love doesn't exist, then I misspoke. Love exists, sort of. Love is like those subatomic neutrinos that exist and don't exist at the same time. Love is a thing but it's also a wave. But it also doesn't exist the moment you look at it."

"Jesus," said Ricardo. "I need to bring two bottles of wine when I come here."

"That would be okay too," said the old man.

Ricardo was quiet for a moment. One of the things he liked about these nightly visits is that the old man made him think.

"Well, I guess as a metaphor for love, that's not bad," Ricardo said aloud, as he mulled it over. "Love does seem like something that slips through your fingers when you try to look at directly."

"Exactly!" the old man exclaimed, "and do you know why that is?"

"Okay... why?" Ricardo asked.

The old man looked to his right and then to his left, then leaned in a bit toward Ricardo. "The Giant Fly explained it all to me. He explained that love really is a type of neutrino. It's made up small atomic particles that float around, and if you inhale enough of them, you feel in love. And these neutrinos are attracted to each other, like swarms of tiny mosquitoes... they hover in the air together, like a fog. He said that's why people fall in love with each other—they've wandered into the same fog patch, and they assume it's the other person that they're in love with. It's also why people fall in love with idiots and thugs—they just happen to be in the same fog. He also explained to me that these love neutrinos actually have a smell—that is, if you were sensitive enough, you could walk into a room, walk around and smell where they were, and just stand in that spot, waiting for someone else to walk into the same neutrino patch, and that's how people 'fall in love'. Pretty amazing, huh? People kinda know that there is a smell to love, that's why they keep trying to make perfumes—they think the smell is the cause of love, but of course, people are wrong. The smell of love is just the byproduct of the love neutrino, not the cause of love."

Ricardo just stared at the old man. He never knew if he was in the presence of a mental patient or a genius poet. Finally he asked, "And why do people fall out of love?"

"Most times they don't," the old man explained. "They get tired of the real life actual person... but if the neutrinos stay in their bodies, they can always feel love. It's just that most people let anger, pettiness, and external events harden them. And sometimes they just don't need to be with that particular person. But you know how they are—they'll go out and try again."

"Yeah, I know that," Ricardo said.

"There is one thing though," the old man continued. "One thing The Giant Fly also told me. He said that there was a wave that the love neutrinos avoided. The Giant Fly didn't have a name for it, but he said that when that particular wavelength was active, the love neutrinos fled as fast as they could."

"Was this another type of neutrino?" Ricardo asked.

"No, it was just a wave, like a sound wave... or maybe a magnetic wave. The Giant Fly was quite clear that this wave was not a particle like a neutrino; it was a wave, something that scattered the love neutrinos the moment it appeared. But that's all he told me. I asked what it was called, and he said he didn't know."

"Maybe it's an 'anti-love' wave," Ricardo said with a smile, "or some type of negative energy."

"No, no that was the weird part," the old man replied. "The Giant Fly didn't treat it like a negative thing at all. In fact, he talked about it in glowing terms, as if it was a positive thing."

Chapter 11: Sex

Miguel was waiting for Ricardo in the locker room inside the bathhouse. He had already stripped down and was simply sitting on one of the benches with a towel wrapped around his waist when Ricardo entered.

Ricardo paid the entrance fee at the counter, took the towel and the small padlock and key that the clerk handed him, and walked back to the locker room to change.

"Ah, mi amigo," said Miguel, "you're right on time, as usual. You have no idea what a rare thing that is in my country."

Although Miguel was Panamanian, he had an abhorrence of his fellow countrymen's lack of punctuality. It was one of his common complaints about running a restaurant.

"These young men come to me begging for a job as a waiter," he had once complained to Ricardo. "They promise that if I hire them, they will be the most excellent employee ever. So I hire them, but then they show up an hour late the first day! And when I reprimand them, they look at me as if I was crazy, as if it was no big deal."

Miguel was the closest thing that Ricardo had to a friend in Panama. They had met years ago, and had been lovers for a while, but then evolved to being cruising buddies in the bathhouse. This gave them each someone to talk to, and to hang out with, and someone to commiserate with, while they waited for potential sex partners to stroll by.

"How are you my friend?" Miguel asked as Ricardo was starting to get undressed. "You seem preoccupied."

"Sorry," Ricardo answered, "I guess I am. I don't know why. I had a friend email me from the states this morning—she's having work problems."

"Does she work in a restaurant?" Miguel asked.

91

"No, no she doesn't."

"Well, then she should count her blessings."

"Ha, well, she might be better off working in a restaurant," Ricardo said. "I don't know why it bothers me so, you know, maybe she's just the kind of person I worry about. I can't do anything about it—she's two thousand miles away."

"That makes it tough to help," agreed Miguel. "How are you otherwise?"

"I'm okay, I guess. How about you?"

"Knee deep in problems, my friend. That's why I come here, to escape from work for just a few hours."

Ricardo knew there were other reasons Miguel came to the bathhouse, but his comment about work made Ricardo think back to his life in the United States, when he too couldn't wait to get off work.

"I understand," he said to Miguel.

"The trouble with running a restaurant, though, is that you can never really leave it behind!" Miguel exclaimed. "I think about it day and night. Even now, I worry about it."

Ricardo put the last of his clothes in the locker, closed the door and secured it with the padlock, wrapped his towel around him, and said to Miguel, "Come on my friend, let's go into the steam room and see if the heat will evaporate both of our worries."

Ricardo was right about the steam room and the effect of steam on his body and mind. He loved the way that it melted all his thoughts and seemed to relax his muscles. He had visited many bathhouses in many countries but he was particularly fond of this one in La Chorrera. Unlike some bathhouses that installed a small steam room as a necessity to earn the title of bathhouse, this particular bathhouse had made the steam room the center of its operation. The steam room was big, and the large tile steps for sitting were designed so that Ricardo could comfortably sit, lean back, stretch out, and just take in the whole scene. There was just enough light from the small overhead bulbs to make out the forms of naked men, their towels casually thrown over their shoulders, as they wandered in and walked around a bit to see who else was there (and to exhibit themselves) and found a place to sit. Off to one side of this center room, there were several dark corners where men could retreat if they wanted a bit of privacy, but most men simply did their thing right in the open, allowing everyone else to watch and enjoy.

Miguel and Ricardo walked in and found places to sit, about six feet away from a heavy-set man who was receiving a blowjob from a younger man. Six feet was about the optimal distance in the heavy steam to get a good view of any action without intruding unnecessarily. Anyone wishing to get involved would, of course, sit closer.

But Miguel and Ricardo sat a bit away. Miguel folded his towel up to sit on, exposing his body to anyone who walked by, a signal that he was open to play. Ricardo sat with his towel still wrapped around him, signaling that for the moment, he was only observing. He leaned back, resting his back on the warm tile step behind him, stretched his arms out to either side, took in a deep breath, and gazed over at the blowjob still in progress.

He looked at the heavy-set man who was receiving the blowjob. The fact was, the man was more than just heavy—he was fat. His head was bald but his chest, shoulders and back were covered with copious amounts of black hair. Ricardo guessed his age at about forty-five years old. The man giving him the blowjob was much younger. Ricardo couldn't see his face because the fellow was down on his knees, in between the older man's thick legs, going up and down on the older man's cock. One of his arms rested on the older man's thigh; the other hand was playing with the older man's balls. Ricardo couldn't see his face but guessed his age at twenty, maybe twenty-five. But from where he was sitting, Ricardo could get a glimpse of the older man's cock, as the younger man went up and down on it. The cock was large, thick and dark.

That's the thing about bathhouses, Ricardo thought. They are the great equalizers. Ricardo looked at the older man again. He was short... a short, fat, balding, relatively unattractive man. Ricardo imagined him in a suit, going to a bar after work, trying to pick someone up—man or woman. He imagined him on vacation, lounging by the hotel pool, trying to talk to any nearby women, and being rebuffed by all of them. He would have worse luck at the gay bars, which cater in their not-so-subtle way to younger gay men. No, the bathhouse was the great equalizer, especially if someone had a nice cock. Because the cock was all that mattered in the bathhouse. The nakedness and the steam stripped away all forms of status, presentation, and pretense. With a little patience, even the ugliest man in the world could get a blowjob in a bathhouse. Ricardo knew that the young man probably never even looked at the older man's face—he just saw that large cock, got down on his knees and took it greedily into his mouth. For those men who enjoyed giving blowjobs, well, the bathhouse was their cornucopia, or perhaps, Ricardo smiled to himself, it should be called a cockucopia.

Ricardo was no different than any other man, gay or straight: he enjoyed giving head as well as receiving it. He knew that even the most ardent self-proclaimed straight man secretly longed to suck another man's cock, to feel that smooth head and shaft all in his mouth and jammed down his throat. But Ricardo simply never gave head in the bathhouses. Even though the risk of contracting HIV was infinitesimally small for anyone giving head, Ricardo refused to take that chance with strangers. Besides, there were plenty of other diseases besides HIV to consider when blowing a stranger in a bathhouse: Hepatitis C, gonorrhea of the throat, even TB, depending on whoever else had just recently sucked that same man.

It was odd, Ricardo thought, because he had never been averse to going down on women the first time he got them into bed. In fact, he relished it. Well, no, he then thought, that wasn't true. He never would go down on prostitutes for the same reason he never would give head in the bathhouse. But then, of course, he remembered, he did go down on Magali. Ricardo started thinking about the different types of sex. It must be, he thought, that sex in a bathhouse is just sex—it's just the feeling of flesh, especially a hard cock, totally separate from the person, whoever they are, whose cock you are touching. And that was true in the brothels—it was just the feeling of flesh. But maybe meeting a woman in a bar or somewhere else, striking up a conversation, getting to know her, somehow mutually deciding in that unspoken way to have sex—all that required a large amount of attraction, a sufficient amount of energy, lust, and curiosity to overcome the fear of rejection. There is no fear of rejection in a bathhouse. If you approach someone and they signal no, you just move on to the next person. Feelings about rejection never come into play, the same way that attractiveness doesn't come into play in the bathhouse. The men cycle through the steam room or the dark rooms or the corridors, endlessly cruising until someone's availability matches up to someone's willingness, and the sucking or fucking or handjobs begin. Likewise, there's no risk of rejection in a brothel. That's what you're paying for—you're paying to eliminate the risk of rejection. But meeting someone outside of the bathhouse or the brothel, talking to them, finding common ground, recognizing a mutual attraction, flirting, giving and receiving signals, the subtle touching, the maneuvering of getting them back to one's apartment—that requires a certain energy, a very different sexual energy. Somehow trust comes into play... trust and caring. In those situations where he cared, Ricardo was much more concerned with the woman's pleasure than his own. He relished going down on them, because he knew that so few men did it well, so few men were as enthusiastic about it as he was, so few men took their time. Ricardo knew that if he could bring that woman to orgasm with his mouth, she would be his, at least in that brief moment.

Besides, Ricardo enjoyed the sensation of eating pussy. He liked the softness of the lips, the joy of gently causing the clit to swell, the taste, the soft hair on the woman who didn't shave or wax, the rising of the flesh around the pussy... he enjoyed everything about it. Fucking was good too, of course, but fucking involved some work, whereas eating pussy was just a pure joy.

That must be it, he thought, something about the relationship with the woman changed the dynamics of sex. And, as he thought back through the years, he realized that this was also true of men with whom he had had relationships. With those men whom he had gotten to know, to trust, he enjoyed going down on them.

But that thought led to a sad realization about how few relationships there had been in recent years. He had had Miguel, Ali, and Magali, and there was that brief affair with a friend of Miguel's a few years back. But for all his years in Panama, he only had those four people as lovers. And while there had been many other partners in Panama, they were all either prostitutes or men in bathhouses. He had to reach back through the years, to his previous life in the states, to find someone that he had cared about and who had, for whatever brief period, cared about him.

Ricardo thought about these things as he sat in the steam room, watching the wisps of steam swirl around the young man sucking the thick cock of the older fat man. Only fifteen minutes had gone by since Ricardo had entered the bathhouse to meet Miguel, and already time had stopped again, and Ricardo was simply in the moment.

The fat man began to breathe heavier, and Ricardo could see him starting to thrust his pelvis in and out of the younger man's mouth. He reached his fat arms around and grabbed both sides of the younger man's head, keeping the head forced down on his cock. The younger man began to gag a bit and tried to push himself up off the cock, but the fat man held him firm. Then the fat man gave out a series of grunts, more like small bellows, and pushed his pelvis up and held it there. A giant whale, Ricardo thought, blowing fluid out of his blowhole. Then the fat man's arms fell to his side, and the younger man was free to quickly pull his head up off the still-erect cock, thick and glistening in the soft light. The younger man stood up, spat a huge glob of cum out on the floor, took in a quick gulp of air, and spat out another wad of cum and then walked quickly out of the steam room. The fat man just slouched against the tile steps, his arms immobile at his side, his head resting on his chest, breathing heavily. Ricardo watched the fat man's cock gradually soften and bend to one side, finally falling over, like a wounded soldier giving up the fight. Finally the fat man slowly stood up, wrapped his towel around him, holding it closed by the two corners as it didn't quite cover his girth, and he lumbered out of the steam room, no doubt, Ricardo thought, to the showers.

Yes, the bathhouse may be a playhouse for young men. But it's a special blessing for unattractive older men. Where else would they get sex? The thought depressed him a bit, as he thought about his own life. He was lucky to have known Ali and lucky to have found Magali, but he knew why he felt lucky—it was because the years had slipped by, and finding lovers was simply getting harder and harder. When he was in his twenties and thirties, he would never have felt the appreciation for luck in finding a women that he felt now, because they were so plentiful back then. He had been handsome as a young man, and while he was not unhandsome now, women of the type and age who appealed to him were no longer interested in him. He didn't like to think about it, but he was an older man now. A "silver fox" as Ali liked to call him, but she was being kind, as only women can be. Ricardo wondered if he would ever meet another woman like Ali or Magali again. He thought about Carolina for a minute, but knew that she was too young to ever think of him as someone other than a friend or mentor. Only time would tell, Ricardo thought. Time and luck, and everyone is entitled to a little bit of luck. In the meantime, while he waited, there was Jenny's and there was the bathhouse. Thank God for both of them.

Ricardo looked over to his left. About twenty feet away, it appeared that someone had someone else bent over one of the large tile steps, and was fucking him from behind. There was too much steam to see clearly at that distance. The steam seemed to suck all the color out of the scene, and Ricardo could only make out the two silhouettes, both standing but with one man in front bent at the waist, supporting himself with his arms on the tile step, while the other silhouette stood behind him, arms grasping both hips of the man in front, thrusting in and out. There was no sound, only the soft hiss of steam that swirled around them, softening their shapes and turning them into a ghostly cartoon, like an eighteenth-century French shadow play.

That was another thing Ricardo liked about the steam room—it was like a theatre that never stopped showing an endless array of steamy soft black and white vignettes, coupling and uncoupling, a constant rearranging of bodies, space, and separateness.

A man walked by Ricardo but paused in front of Miguel. Miguel reached up and stroked the man's thigh. The man was uncircumcised, and had a nice long cock. Miguel began playing with it. The man glanced down at the space between Miguel and Ricardo, and Ricardo scooted over to give the man a place to sit. As the man sat down, Ricardo undraped his own towel, exposing himself. The man began playing with Miguel's cock with his right hand and playing with Ricardo's cock with his left hand. Miguel was stroking the man's cock, which now was getting erect, the pink head emerging from its hood. Ricardo leaned back, closed his eyes, and let the feeling of being touched and fondled fill him with a pleasant sad joy.

The man spent several lovely minutes sitting there, masturbating them both, before he stood up and moved on to play with other men. Both Miguel and Ricardo were hard now.

"He was nice looking," Miguel said.

"Yes he was," Ricardo answered, although in fact Ricardo had barely looked at the man.

"Perhaps we'll see him again," Miguel added.

By now, Miguel and Ricardo had been in the steam for almost half an hour.

"Do you want to go sit in the hot tub for a while?" Miguel asked.

"Good idea," Ricardo said.

And they both got up and found their way out of the steam room.

Chapter 12: Money

One of the last things that Ricardo did on the day in question, sometime after his Skype conversation with Carolina, but before he went to bed, was to open up his laptop and take a quick look at his finances. He had made the offer to give Carolina some money if she needed it, and he wanted to double check his accounts to see that there was enough there to make good on his offer in case she did in fact need it.

Ricardo kept a savings account in a Panamanian bank. He knew there would not be much money there, but out of habit, he checked that balance first. That was the account where the US Social Security Administration directly deposited his monthly Social Security check, and that was the money that Ricardo used each month to live on. There was rarely much left by the end of the month. But Ricardo had two other accounts back in the states: one was a savings account where a small deposit was made each month by a pension fund he had with his former law firm employer. It wasn't much of a pension, but it accumulated because Ricardo only dipped into it when he needed to fly back to the States. His other stateside account was an investment account that he kept as back-up, a safety net, and he had not touched that account for many years. He had created it decades earlier from a small inheritance he had received from his grandfather. At the time he created it, the stock market was booming, and back then Ricardo hoped he would retire with a comfortable nest egg. But the crash of 2008 almost wiped it out. It was one of the reasons that moving to Panama quickly became his only retirement option if he truly wished to retire and write. He switched brokers, instructing the new broker to only invest conservatively, and had left that account alone since

2008, and had watched it slowly start to inch back up. It was nowhere near where it was at its height, but at least there was a bit of a safety net there now.

He looked at the current balance in that account and concluded that he could afford to give Carolina a few thousand dollars if in fact she did quit or get fired. It gave him some comfort to think that he could help her if she needed it.

"And why did you lose so much money?" the old man had asked him one time after Ricardo had shared the story about receiving an inheritance from his grandfather and deciding to invest it.

"I told you. The stock market took a huge nosedive. My investments were suddenly worth less than half of what they were once worth."

"What were your investments in?" the old man asked.

"Mutual funds."

"What were those mutual funds invested in?" the old man pressed.

"I don't know exactly," Ricardo answered. "Supposedly, they were spread out, invested in a wide array of stocks and bonds."

"But you don't know what stocks or bonds they held?"

"No."

"Uh huh," the old man said, while rubbing his chin. "And why did you pick mutual funds?"

"They were supposed to be safe," Ricardo answered.

"I see," said the old man. "Well, you are no different than most gringos I have met. You had money and no fucking clue what to do with it. So some salesman told you that XYZ was a good investment and so you gave him your money. You don't even know what you were invested in. You're lucky you didn't lose it all."

Ricardo thought the old man's words were harsh, but he had gotten used to his abrasiveness. Besides, he couldn't disagree with his analysis.

"Pretty much," was all Ricardo could say.

"Well," the old man continued, "do you remember the

story about the rich man and his three servants? The one where the rich man is going away for a trip so he entrusts each of his servants with some money? And the first servant simply invests all of his share and makes a huge return; and the second servant uses his money to open a business and works hard, and makes a decent return on the money; but the third servant just buries his money in the ground and does nothing with it. Do you remember this story? You should—it's in the Bible."

"Yeah, yeah, I remember it," Ricardo said. "The the rich man returns and he rewards the first two servants, but he fires the third servant. What about it?"

"Well, *first* he takes back all the money the third servant had buried in the ground, and *then* he fires him and throws him out of the house, basically making him homeless," the old man said.

"Okay, and your point?" Ricardo asked.

"My point, don Ricardo, is that the Bible got it wrong. Most of you gringos would have been better off burying your money in the ground rather than investing it. I mean, the Bible was basically praising the person who took the most investment risks."

Ricardo thought about this a minute. "I never thought about it that way, but yeah, you're right. I certainly would have been better off just putting my inheritance in a bank. The last ten years in the stock market have been rough."

"Rough?" exclaimed the old man, "don't you mean *fraudulent*?"

"Are you talking about all that subprime stuff?"

"That and more," the old man said.

"Well, I know that there were a lot of accusations of fraud... and I think some people went to jail. But all that stock market stuff is kinda beyond me."

"Yet you invested in it?" the old man said and smiled.

"Well, what else was I supposed to do with it?" Ricardo asked.

"Bury it in the ground!" the old man exclaimed. "If there's one thing I've learned, it's that if the Bible tells you *not to do* something, that's the one thing you *should* do."

Ricardo laughed, and reached for the Sangria bottle and refilled the old man's glass.

"Gracias, mi amigo," the old man said. "Do you know, don Ricardo, how that parable with the three servants would have been written if the Bible was actually telling the truth?"

"How?" Ricardo asked.

"Well, back when that story was written, Mesopotamia was a hotbed of olive trading. Olive oil was in huge demand. Everyone in Egypt, Canaan, and Persia wanted it. So, the first servant would have invested all his money into an olive oil business, and he would made a nice little profit, enough to buy himself a little house. But the olive oil market would have kept booming, and the first servant was greedy, so he would have gone to Sol the lender and gotten a loan on his little house. Then he would have taken that money and gone to some farmers and bought next year's harvest of olives in advance. And because the price of olive oil continued to go up, his contracts for next year's harvests would have been worth a lot. So he would have used those contracts as collateral to borrow more money from Sol to buy more contracts, but this time he would have bought olive oil production contracts from the olive oil trading houses, on their future production, and he would have only put ten percent down on these production contracts, and the olive oil trading houses would have loaned him the rest. When the other two servants saw how much money the first servant was worth, the second servant cashed in all his investments and bought olive oil future productions contracts as well, and the third servant dug up his money and did the same. Meanwhile, Sol was loaning money like crazy, and he was a little cash poor, but the loan business was great, so he bundled up all his little loans, and sold shares of them to some investors. They in turn sold them to other investors. The first servant didn't even know who owned his mortgage anymore. When all the olive farmers in Mesopotamia had sold all their future harvests, the olive oil trading houses didn't have any more real future production contracts to sell. So they made up a product called an olive oil index. It was basically a bet that the price of olive oil would continue to go up, but it wasn't backed by any real olive oil—it was just a bet. But it was real popular, and all three servants bought them up like crazy. Even Sol bought some from his profits from selling his loans. But then Sol started to get worried that maybe the price of olive oil would fall, so he took out some insurance from a guy named Ebrahim... you know, just to hedge his bet a little. If the price of olive oil fell, the insurance was supposed to cover Sol's losses. Well, Sol didn't know it, but Ebrahim was selling insurance to everyone under the table, to the other two servants and even to the olive oil trading houses. Nobody knew it, but everyone had insurance with Ebrahim. Are you with me so far, don Ricardo?"

"No," said Ricardo, laughing, "but keep going."

"Well, *then* of course, Arabia figured out how to mix vegetable oil with ghee." The old man paused, looked at Ricardo, and asked, "You do know what ghee is, don't you, don Ricardo?"

"No," said Ricardo, between laughs. "I don't."

The old man shook his head. "Ghee is a type of clarified butter, very popular in Arabia. Anyway, Arabia figured out how to mix cheap vegetable oil with ghee, and it tasted pretty good and cost only a fraction of what olive oil cost, and Arabia started marketing this new oil like crazy, and it started selling, and the olive oil market started to crumble. The olive oil trading houses started calling in their margins and of course the three servants were so overextended, they couldn't pay, so they lost everything. Ebrahim couldn't pay all the insurance claims, so he went bankrupt. Sol went bankrupt. All the people who borrowed money from Sol—and that turned out to be everybody—well, they couldn't pay. So all the loans that Sol had sold to all the investors were now worthless. Then the master who had given the three servants the money originally, well he came home, found out what had happened, and he killed the three servants; Sol killed Ebrahim; and the investors who lost money on Sol's loans came by one night and killed Sol. *That's* how the parable of the three servants would have read if the Bible was telling the truth."

Ricardo was still laughing. "That's a pretty fantastic

story," he said.

"Fantastic?" exclaimed the old man. "Do you think it's farfetched?"

"Well, yeah, but it's funny," Ricardo answered.

"Really?" said the old man, "really?" The old man stared at Ricardo for a moment. "Tell me, don Ricardo, do you know what caused *your* market to crash?"

"Um... well no... I mean, there were a lot of exposés at the time about Wall Street greed and all those subprime loans, and I know a lot of banks failed, but do I really know what *caused* it all to crash? No, I would have to say I don't."

"Uh huh... uh huh..." the old man said with a sigh. "Well, señor gringo, since you think *my* story is so fantastic, and also because you are so kind to bring me Sangria every night, I will tell you how *your* market crashed."

There was a more serious tone in the old man's voice now. Ricardo sat back in his chair and listened.

"Your subprime loan scandal didn't *cause* the crash, but it was a part of it," the old man began. "And the crash wasn't a crash—it was more like a bomb that had five different fuses all burning at the same time. You might call it a capital bomb. One of the fuses was all those bad real estate loans, and that fuse was lit back in the late 1970s when all you... you... what do you gringos call yourselves? Oh yeah, baby boomers... stupid name, but anyway, all you baby boomers were all grown up, and you all wanted to own a home, just like your parents had. All of you were raised on your so-called American Dream, you know. So you all started going to the banks to get loans to buy a house, because part of that American Dream was that borrowing money is a good thing. Ha! We don't have that crazy delusion down here because poverty is in our blood, but you gringos think debt is freedom. So you all went to your banks. But your banks didn't have any money to lend because they were under strict rules that were put in place after your Great Depression. They had to keep a certain amount of reserve capital on hand, so once they had made a certain number of loans, and put aside a certain amount of capital to cover *those* loans, they simply didn't have any money left over to lend. So here you had all these baby boomers clamoring to buy houses, and there was no money to lend. So everyone started crying to Congress. Are you with me so far?"

"Yeah," Ricardo said, and then asked, "And how do you know all this?"

"The same reason I know about olive oil," the old man said. "The Giant Fly told me. So anyway, your Congress had this agency... well, it wasn't really an agency; it was actually a corporation, called Fannie Mae. But it looked like a federal agency, and everyone thought it was a federal agency, and its job was to buy up loans from banks. Because that's how your government created money for banks to make new loans—Fannie Mae would buy up a bank's loans, and the bank would take the money from that sale and use it to make more loans. Plus the banks made fees from selling the mortgages to new homeowners and fees for selling the mortgages to Fannie Mae. The banks had a nice little business going, but they weren't getting rich, because they had to abide by all these regulations. For example, they could only sell mortgages to Fannie Mae that were good credit risks, and Fannie Mae had strict rules about that. But even with Fannie Mae buying up the bank mortgages, there still wasn't enough money to loan to all you baby boomers. So people were still crying to Congress, and that included poor people, who also wanted their piece of your American Dream. And the banks were also crying to Congress for more money and less regulation.

"Now at some point, Fannie Mae had bought up so many loans, they were out of money. But they had all these good credit mortgages, so they pressured Congress to rewrite the rules so that *they* could sell the mortgages, and Congress obliged, and do you know who Fannie Mae sold their mortgages to?"

Ricardo had stopped smiling and was listening intently. Unlike many of the old man's wild stories, this one actually had a ring of truth to it, and Ricardo was interested. "No," he said, "who?"

"To Wall Street, señor, who else? And of course, Fannie Mae made a nice little profit on that. You do understand how you can sell a debt like a mortgage, don't you?"

"Well, that's all a bond is, right? A promise to pay, just like a mortgage," Ricardo said.

"Exactly. But what Fannie Mae did, to make the mortgages attractive to Wall Street, was to *securitize* them, that is, Fannie Mae guaranteed the principal and the payments. And because people believed Fannie Mae was a government agency—which it wasn't—it made these mortgages attractive to Wall Street, because Wall Street could package these mortgages up and sell them to investors as safe investments. And, in fact they were pretty safe, because Fannie Mae only bought good credit risk mortgages from the banks. So anyway, that was one fuse to this capital bomb. Investors got used to buying these safe mortgage-backed securities. The second fuse was close by. There were a lot of baby boomers who weren't good credit risks. And there were a lot of people who might have been good credit risks, but they were low-income folks. And there were a lot of people in your Congress who wanted to free up capital for those folks, and why? Because those folks voted. So, there was a lot of pressure building up to make loans to less than prime candidates. But the banks couldn't do that, because they were so heavily regulated. But the independent mortgage companies could, *if* they could find a way to sell the mortgages. So it was just a matter of time before someone figured out that you could bundle up a couple of these crappy mortgages with some good mortgages and still sell them to investors. As long as Fannie Mae was guaranteeing their own mortgages, a few crappy ones wouldn't hurt the mix. But then Wall Street started to wonder if there wasn't some way to increase the mix. Well, I shouldn't use the term Wall Street... it's too broad... But there were these investment banks on Wall Street—and I've never understood why they were called banks, because they are just investment companies—but nonetheless, these investment banks wondered if there was a way they could increase the mix of these crappy mortgages, and that when they lit the third fuse to the capital bomb— the accountants."

"Wait a minute," Ricardo interrupted. "The Giant Fly told you all this?"

"Well, no, not exactly," the old man explained. "The Giant Fly told me how your gringo economy was like a bomb with five fuses all burning at once, and how all five fuses hit the bomb at exactly the same time... but I had to figure out what the fuses were."

"And how did you do that?" Ricardo asked.

"Well, I'm old and I've been around," the old man answered. "You think that market speculation is a new thing? Just invented for your generation? Ha! Remember the tulip market crash of 1637?"

"The what?"

"The tulip market crash of 1637. Shit, don't they teach you gringos anything in school? Tulips from Holland were real popular in the early 1600s, and the tulip growers in Holland started selling futures. You do know what futures are, don't you?"

"Of course," Ricardo answered. "You agree to pay a price today to buy something in the future."

"Right... well, a bunch of investors started selling bets on the rising future price of tulips back in 1637. They didn't even own the tulip bulbs or the futures contracts. They were just selling bets that the price of tulips would continue to go up. And because the prices *were* going up, people bought those investments like crazy, hoping to make a fast buck. Made no sense to me—I don't even like tulips, but they were real popular back then and people had money, so they speculated. It was the first case of flower power... ha ha ha."

The old man started laughing. He had the kind of laugh that was contagious, and it made Ricardo smile.

"So what happened?" Ricardo asked.

"Well, the bubble collapsed, of course. And by then the tulip market was selling synthetic derivatives of tulip futures, just like how the olive oil trading houses were selling olive oil indexes in Mesopotamia, so millions of dollars were lost. People were wiped out. But of course, people never learn and it just takes one generation to grow up and they do it all over again.

Ricardo started to feel agitated. "Wait a minute–synthetic what?" he asked.

107

"Synthetic derivatives... but I'll get to those later. I was talking about the accountants, the third fuse of your capital bomb. You see, the nice thing about the Fannie Mae mortgages was that they were highly rated, because they were in fact pretty safe. And someone realized that if someone else could give a safe rating to these crappy mortgages, then they could sell them as an investment the same way they sold the Fannie Mae mortgages. Now, this is totally unrelated to mortgages. But at the same time all this real estate crap was happening, the huge accounting companies were pressuring Congress to deregulate them. Up to that point, accounting companies had to keep an arm's length relationship with businesses that they audited... you know, for *ethical* reasons. But many of them soon realized they could make more money *advising* these companies than they could by simply *auditing* them. Remember Enron and Arthur Anderson?"

"Well, yes I do, but how do *you* know this shit?

"I'm an old man, and I've been around. Anyway, you remember that Enron was paying Arthur Anderson millions of dollars to help them cook the books, so that Arthur Anderson would certify their annual reports so that Enron could keep their stock prices high and keep that investor money flowing in?"

"I never did understand how all those auditors lied like that," Ricardo said.

The old man looked at Ricardo. "I'm trying to explain it to you, don Ricardo. Everyone is greedy; everyone has their price; and when it comes to organizations, you only have to buy off a small percentage of key people before you corrupt the whole organization. Enron bought off the Arthur Anderson employees who worked the Enron account, and then those auditors were making so much money for the Arthur Anderson company that the management team at Arthur Anderson wasn't going to jeopardize that! So the entire auditing firm of Arthur Anderson went along with Enron. And then when other accounting firms saw how much money Arthur Anderson was making by their so-called *consulting*, then they wanted to get into the consulting business as well. Pretty soon all the accounting firms pressured Congress to allow them to consult with clients, which pretty much meant the clients were telling the auditors how to do the audits. But I digress. My point was that it didn't take much to get some of these auditing firms to start stamping those subprime loans as grade AAA investments."

"Well, how could they do that? I mean, how could they just say a bad mortgage was a good credit risk?" Ricardo asked.

"Ah, that brings me to the fourth fuse: insurance companies. With these crappy mortgages, Wall Street would simply buy insurance policies guaranteeing that the bad mortgage wouldn't fail, so theoretically there was no risk. The auditors, you know, for a small fee, would stamp the investment grade AAA, and Wall Street could sell them. They didn't have to mix them in with good Fannie Mae loans. They just had to grab a bunch of mortgages, get a good rating, and give them an official sounding name, and they sold like hotcakes."

"Well, weren't the insurance companies regulated? I mean, how could they just sell insurance on bad mortgages?" Ricardo asked.

"Well, they were regulated in terms of traditional insurance policies for individuals, like accident insurance or car insurance, but these mortgage-backed securities were such a new product, that there were no regulations. And besides, every time someone tried to regulate them, the lobbyists from Wall Street would descend on Congress and bribe enough congressmen to kill any regulations."

"Bribe them?" Ricardo asked.

"Well, sorry, make a campaign contribution... but basically they bought off your Congress. All the regulations that your government had put in place after your stock market crash of 1929 were repealed. When everybody is making money, no one wants regulation. Anyway, that brings me to the fifth fuse—foreign markets. All this stuff in your country was happening at exactly the same time that there was a ton of new money in Europe. The European Union was being formed and the countries that wanted into the Eurozone had to show they didn't have much debt. So they bought these credit default swaps and showed them on their books as a credit..."

Ricardo's head hurt. "Wait a minute," he said, "I don't understand credit default swaps."

"Ha! Neither did they. In fact, nobody does. But let's just say it was the way that Spain, Italy, and Greece bought their way into the Eurozone. They bought these credit default swaps, which were basically bad bets, and they put them on their books as a credit. It would be like you going to the horse race and betting twenty dollars on a fifty-to-one long shot but then writing in your checkbook that you made one hundred dollars even before the race started. It looks good on paper. And of course, once they got into the European Union, the Eurozone banks loaned them tons of money, so they invested it into all these synthetic derivatives."

"Wait! Stop!" exclaimed Ricardo. "What are those?"

The old man looked at Ricardo, shook his head, and then said, "Well, a derivative is something whose value is derived from something else. Remember the tulips? Well, suppose I'm a tulip grower and you pay me twenty dollars for the option of buying one hundred tulips from me for ten dollars each. I'm not selling you the tulips now. And you may decide not to buy them. But you have the *option* of buying them for ten dollars each. The value of that option is *derived* from the value of the tulips. That option is a derivative. So maybe you think the value of tulips will go down but someone else thinks they will go up. So you sell your option to that person for thirty dollars, and you have a nice ten dollars profit. That's a real derivative. But maybe you don't own the option, but you still think the price of tulips will go down, so you make up a fake or synthetic option, and you sell it to someone for thirty dollars. Now you've made thirty dollars. And it's not illegal, because you tell them in the tiny print somewhere that it's a fake or synthetic derivative."

"Why would anyone buy that?" Ricardo asked.

The old man started laughing. "Oh, don Ricardo... they bought them by the millions! By the fucking millions! In Mesopotamia, and Holland, and New York, London, Iceland, Paris, everywhere. And you did too. If you go back and dig

110

through those precious mutual funds that you lost money on, you would find that you owned synthetic derivatives. Ha ha! The Giant Fly said it best: he told me that 'people are the most stupid when they are greedy', and The Giant Fly is always right."

The old man broke into another fit of laughter. Ricardo reached over to the table and refilled his own glass with Sangria, then sat back and watched the old man laugh. Ricardo did not know if anything the old man had said was true, but he was once again amazed at the old man's ability to talk in depth about a subject. As far as Ricardo knew, the old man had never left Panama, had never gotten further than high school. Ricardo realized that he didn't know what the old man had done for a living. In fact, Ricardo knew very little about the old man. He just liked listening to him talk.

When the old man had stopped laughing, Ricardo asked, "So you're saying that all five of these fuses all ignited this bomb at the same time, like some perfect storm of events, and then the bomb exploded and that's what caused the financial crash?"

"Well, yes, it exploded and then it reset, like it always does."

"What do you mean, it reset?" Ricardo asked.

"Well, that's how investments work, don Ricardo, they're just like the beautiful casinos in Panama City. You make up a game for the rubes to bet on, and you take all their money. Once all their money is gone, you have to come up with a brand new game. The bomb exploded and then it reset with five new fuses."

"What are you talking about?" Ricardo asked.

"Well, nothing changed. Your Congress didn't pass any new regulations. Subprime mortgages still exist; synthetic derivatives are still sold; credit is still cheap; the bomb is just reset with new fuses. The only reason that your little investment account is growing in value now is because there are new customers in the casino. Nothing has changed. You said you changed brokers when you lost your money?"

"Yeah."

"And you told him to only make conservative

investments?"

"Right."

"And what is your money invested in now?" the old man asked.

"Some bonds, some mutual funds, some index funds," Ricardo said.

"And what are those mutual funds invested in now?" the old man asked.

Ricardo saw too late where this was going. "I don't know exactly," he admitted.

"You see?" the old man smiled almost sympathetically. "Nothing has changed."

"And what would you recommend I do with that money, señor?" Ricardo asked.

"Well, you could do what I do," the old man replied.

"And what is that?" Ricardo asked.

"Well, I bury my money in the ground, of course. Ha ha ha! Just like The Giant Fly tells me to. After breaking into a cackle, he then said, "Would you be so kind, don Ricardo, to go to the icebox and bring me some fresh ice?"

Ricardo got up, still thinking about the old man's words, and went into the kitchen and retrieved the ice tray. On the way back to the old man, Ricardo noticed a vase on the kitchen counter with two tulips in it.

*   *   *

Ricardo closed his laptop, having assured himself that there was enough money available to give some to Carolina if she needed it. Bits and pieces of the memory of that long ago conversation with the old man came back to him. The thought crossed his mind that he didn't know any more about what his money was invested now than he did when he had that conversation with the old man. He only hoped that he would always have a little bit of money put aside, enough for him and enough to help the people he loved. He put away his laptop and started thinking about going to bed.

Chapter 13: Walking

As indicated, after Ricardo finished his dinner at the Soda de la Linda, he began the ten-minute walk to the old man's apartment. Walking was something Ricardo enjoyed doing—it was pretty high on his list, right below his morning run, sex at the brothel or the bathhouse and, of course, writing. This was a good thing, because besides buses and taxis, his feet were his only way to get around. He had sold his car when he had left New York, and even though he had obtained a Panamanian driver's license when he had first moved to Panama, he had never bought, or even rented, a car there. It was simply too dangerous to drive in Panama. There were no traffic police; everyone drove like crazy; and no one obeyed traffic signs. A taxi driver had explained it to him when he first arrived in Panama: "We treat the signs as advisory," the driver had said, "not mandatory." Every road was considered a racetrack and every intersection was approached as a game of chicken. Thus, like most gringos who lived in Panama, Ricardo simply found it easier and safer not to drive. Buses and taxis got him anywhere far away that he needed to get to, and Villa Rosario was small enough that he could walk anywhere. Walking, of course, had some of the same risks as driving, because pedestrians had no right of way, regardless of stop signs, traffic lights, or common sense. It was not unheard of for a pedestrian to be struck on the sidewalk by a car simply because the driver chose to pass another car by driving up onto the sidewalk. Thus Ricardo, like all the locals, was ever mindful of all the traffic around him as he walked from downtown on this particular evening. But the evening was pleasant, the air cool, and the walk relaxing.

Because of Panama's proximity to the equator, the time of sunrises and sunsets does not vary with the seasons.

The sun always rose around six in the morning and set around six at night. On the evening in question, as Ricardo walked to the old man's apartment, the sun was just going down behind the hills that surround Villa Rosario, filling the streets and sidewalks with its customary dingy yellow luminescence. As Ricardo walked, he thought about the old man.

For some reason, the old man had been on a kick recently about time and death. Ricardo had simply assumed that the old man's preoccupation with death was because he was so old, and that all old people must feel the closeness of death.

"I think The Giant Fly knows the date of my death," the old man had confided recently. "But he won't tell me."

"Maybe that's for the better," Ricardo had replied. "After all, who wants to know the hour of their death?"

"Ha," said the old man. "Don't you find, don Ricardo, that you work better with a deadline? Don't you always complain about your publisher's deadlines, yet you always manage to produce something in time for him? Deadlines make us work harder. You know, they're not called *dead* lines for nothing."

Both Ricardo and the old man broke out laughing. "Yes," Ricardo laughed, "that's truly the last deadline you face."

"But anyway," the old man continued, "I don't think he should hold out on me. If he knows, he should tell me."

"I don't know about that," Ricardo said, "I wouldn't want to know."

"What would you do if you knew?" the old man asked.

Ricardo thought for a moment. "Well," he said, "if I knew for certain, and there was no way to alter it, I guess I would blow through the rest of my savings, spend every night down at Jenny's...maybe go back and visit Spain..." Ricardo was quiet for a moment, then said, "No, no, that's probably not true. I mean, I'm sure there would be some of that... but no, I think I would probably try to get everything in order, take what little savings I have and give them to someone or someplace who I thought deserved them. You know, señor, I honestly don't know what I would do..."

"Don't you think it's odd, don Ricardo, the fact that since the beginning of time, everyone dies, and every single person we've known has either died or will die, and every single person alive on this earth now will die, and yet... with all these deaths, no one knows what they will do? You take any other field, say building a house... suppose you want to build a good house, and you don't know how, and you have no friends who know how, what do you do? Well, you go down to where someone is building a house and you *watch* them. You watch someone else build a house and you think, yes, I would do that or no, I would that differently... but we don't approach death the same way. No one has ever said, 'My uncle died, and this is how he got his things in order, and this is how he spent his last days, and boy oh boy, when my time comes, that's the way I want to do it. I'm going to go out just like he did, because that's the way to go.' No! Each one of us has to go through it like no one on earth had ever died before. Don't you think that's odd? Don't you think that shows a lack of planning, don Ricardo?"

Ricardo laughed and said, "a lack of planning, yes... but that's the least of it. I suppose it's because we want to live forever."

"Would you?" asked the old man, "would you want to live forever?"

"Hmm," said Ricardo. "Talk about no deadlines... I don't know..."

"Maybe that's why the gods are so pernicious," the old man said, "because they're just so pissed off about living forever and having nothing to do."

"Maybe," Ricardo said. "To live forever... it's quite a thought. They say in forty years or so, they'll have made enough advances in medicine and computers to let people merge with computers and live forever."

"Yes," said the old man, "I know what they say... but they are mistaken. The Giant Fly told me it can't be done. He said that part of the program of life is to die, that's it's coded into our MDNA. He said that no matter how many advances you make in medicine, people will always die."

"Our MDNA? What's that?" Ricardo asked.

"Meta-DNA. It's the DNA underneath our DNA, the MDNA. It's the program of life that creates our DNA. It's housed inside the neutrinos in our body."

"I've never heard of it," Ricardo said.

"That's because it hasn't been discovered yet," said the old man.

"Oh... of course," said Ricardo.

*   *   *

Ricardo reached the outskirts of town. The sidewalk became a dirt path by the side of the road. Ricardo followed it up the hill for another five minutes to where he knew the stone steps would be that led to the old man's apartment. As he walked, he wondered how long the old man would live. He wondered if there would come a day when he would knock on the old man's door and no answer would be forthcoming from within. He wondered what he would do if that ever happened. He told himself he should ask the old man if he had any relatives and ask how to get in touch with them if he needed to. He wondered if the old man would consider that an intrusive question, or whether the old man even had any relatives. Maybe it would be better, Ricardo thought, to ask around first. Maybe he would ask Jenny. She seemed to know everything about everyone, regardless if they were customers or not. Who knows? Maybe the old man had a bunch of family. He made a mental note to ask Jenny the next time he was at her establishment which, he reminded himself, should be soon. He hadn't been with a woman for a few weeks and thought a trip to Jenny's was due.

"You know," the old man told him one time, "Ernest Hemingway believed that each man was allotted a certain number of orgasms. He thought that once you used them all up, your body simply died."

"If that were true, priests would live forever," Ricardo countered.

116

"No, no don Ricardo," the old man laughed, "that is why priests *don't* live forever."

After they both stopped laughing, the old man said, "But really, your Ernest Hemingway believed that, and The Giant Fly said that, in a way, he was right."

"Hmm," said Ricardo. "Like if you stop wanting sex, you might as well die?"

"No, no," explained the old man, "not like that at all. The Giant Fly told me that orgasms were the spirit of life, that at the moment of orgasm, all time stops, and at that moment we have the ability to live forever."

"Did you know," Ricardo asked, "that the French expression for orgasm means 'the little death'?"

"Really?" said the old man, "I did not know that. Damn smart, those French. Because that's true too. The moment of death is like the moment of orgasm. All time stops, and for that brief microsecond, before we transition, we have the ability to live forever."

"How exactly?" asked Ricardo.

"Well, timing is important, of course... but The Giant Fly said that at the moment of orgasm, there is something like a brilliant light... except that it's not a light, but it's full of these special neutrinos. And if we could just breathe it in, take all those neutrinos into our body, we could live forever. But we don't do it because our bodies know the price it would have to pay."

"What do you mean?"

"Well, don Ricardo, do you know why you have never met anyone who lives forever?"

"Ah, because there is no such person?"

"Ha, no, no," the old man laughed. "It's because to live forever means that you have to give up your body. And our bodies don't want to do that. So at the moment of orgasm, for that brief millisecond when we are surrounded by the neutrinos of timeless life, our bodies are overwhelmed by their beauty, but then our bodies realize that to take them in means that it would have to change into something else. So our bodies drag us back down, because our bodies don't want to change. But our spirit does, so we keep going back for more sex. Everything thinks it's our bodies that want sex, but it's really our spirit. And that's why The Giant Fly said that, in a way, your Ernest Hemingway was right, that when your spirit stops wanting sex, the body wins, and starts to die. But the spirit eventually has the last laugh, because when our bodies die, we are again surrounded by those timeless neutrinos, and the spirit is free to take them in without the body holding it back."

"Interesting," said Ricardo, "so there's no way to live forever in this body?"

"Well," said the old man, "you can keep fucking as much as you can. You won't live forever, but you can get a glimpse of it."

"I'll drink to that," said Ricardo.

*   *   *

Ricardo reached the stone steps to the old man's apartment and started his climb. It was short but steep. He got to the old man's door and knocked.

Chapter 14:   Now I Lay Me Down

As Ricardo was preparing for bed that night at the end of the day in question, the financial figures from his stateside accounts were still fresh in his mind. He normally flew back to the States once a year for a brief visit, and he was thinking to himself: *Maybe I should move that trip up a bit, try and see Marta, and visit Carolina.* But he knew that his preference for finding the cheapest possible fare usually put his trip out several more months into the cheaper rainy season. He also knew that over the past few years, the length of his trips back to the States had gotten shorter and shorter, as there were simply less people to visit. That's a sad fact that all expats soon find out when they leave the States: that most of their so-called friends from their old jobs and old life are simply not interested in maintaining contact—that only the few real friends stay in contact, but they too move on with their lives. After his trip north last year, Ricardo had even wondered if it was worth it to keep going back each year. Nonetheless, he made a mental note to himself to check the airline fares tomorrow.

Unbeknownst to Ricardo, however, Marta was thinking about him. She had received the email that he had sent earlier that afternoon. She had read it just a few hours ago, and sat thinking fondly of her old friend Ricardo, remembering how they had met in rehab years ago, how miserable and barren both their lives were back then, how they had supported and comforted each other. She had always been grateful for his support back then and over the years. She remembered how, a few years back, she had been so envious when he had decided to move to Panama. "You'll be living in paradise," she told him whenever he expressed trepidation about the move. She was going to write a response to his email that night, but there was dinner to prepare for her family, so she decided to write him first thing in the morning after the children were off to school.

Also unbeknownst to Ricardo, Carolina was also preparing for bed, feeling better that she had been able to talk with her old friend, still worried about tomorrow, but feeling stronger because of Ricardo's feedback and support. And while she had no intention of taking him up on his offer of money, it was still a comfort to her that he had offered it. Of course, as mentioned, neither she nor Ricardo knew at this point that in fact she would be fired tomorrow, and that she would be crying and talking to Ricardo less than twenty-four hours from now. Nor did she or Ricardo know that while none of her efforts to gain justice from DSHS would prevail, she would find employment again within a month, and true to her intention, she would not have to take the money that Ricardo had offered her. And because she did not know any of these things, and because she was feeling better having talked to Ricardo, she was able to fall asleep.

Also unbeknownst to Ricardo, Magali was also preparing for bed, not to sleep, but to work. She was halfway through her shift at Jenny's and was leading a client back to her room. The client was a middle-aged pudgy German man. Panama was a favorite vacation spot for German tourists, and many of them often found their way to Jenny's. Jenny had once told Magali that they got so many German customers not because Germany didn't have its share of brothels (many of which were bigger and better than Jenny's) but because German men eventually got tired of the tall thin blond German prostitutes and had to have something more exotic, and that the shorter darker Panamanian women fit the bill. Magali didn't care why they came to Jenny's as long as they chose her, because after all, it was just a job and she had to earn enough money to support not only her mother, but her grandmother as well. The German men took longer in bed than the local Panamanian clients, but that was okay because at least the Germans tipped her, which the local men rarely did.

Also unbeknownst to Ricardo, Ali was just waking up. She was in Europe with her current boyfriend, a wealthy art dealer from New Mexico. He was married but evidently his wife was ignorant of his affair with Ali or simply just did not care. He had to fly to Europe to personally select a consignment of art for his gallery in New Mexico, and he had invited Ali to join him. It was morning there, and he had gotten up from the hotel bed early to go buy some pastries at a shop around the corner to bring back to Ali. She was lying in the bed drifting back to sleep, while she waited for him to return. His job and his marriage back in the States did not allow him to see Ali often, but when he did spend time with her, he always pampered her. She did not love him, but he was easy to get along with, was a decent lover, and she did like being pampered. She would not want to spend any more time with him—or any man—than she already did, so it was a good arrangement for both of them. It would be nice to say that on this particular morning, which was Ricardo's evening, that Ali was thinking fondly of Ricardo, but at that moment she was not thinking about him at all, but rather, she was wondering what kind of pastries her married lover would be bringing back to her.

Also unbeknownst to Ricardo, Miguel was still finishing up at the restaurant. There had been a late group of seven for drinks and dinner, which caused a flurry of activity in the kitchen, as everyone pitched in to get the seven dinners prepared and served at the same time. Because one of his wait staff had not shown up for the evening shift, Miguel was already doing double duty as host and waiter. When the late diners showed up without a reservation, he had to do triple-duty to help out with the cooking. But despite the unexpected commotion and extra work, he was pleased, because it had been a slow week, and this one unexpected party would help him make payroll. It was a tough business managing a restaurant, and even though he shared ownership of the restaurant with his brother-in-law, Miguel felt that most of the responsibilities and worries fell to him. But now the late party had left, he had locked the doors, the kitchen had been cleaned up, and he was counting the till. Not a bad evening financially at all. Miguel had always been proud that he was the one successful member of his family. His two other brothers had succumbed to drugs—one was in prison and the other was an addict. Only he had grown up to make his parents proud. They always talked about him to their friends at church. That was one of the reasons Miguel kept his gay life hidden deep in the closet. Of course, this was true of most gay Panamanians, and certainly true of every single one of the gay men at the bathhouse in La Chorrera. No one outside of their gay friends knew they were gay. Miguel had read about how young gay men in the United States lived their lives out in the open, and he wondered how liberating that must feel, but he also knew it would never ever work in Panama. His wife would divorce him. The courts would give the children to her. His brother-in-law would take over the restaurant, and all public opinion would turn against him. No, deep in the closet is where he would stay until he died. He was simply grateful he had the bathhouse and his small circle of gay friends to keep him sane.

Also unbeknownst to Ricardo, the old man, at this very moment, was having an in-depth conversation with The Giant Fly, and they were in fact discussing Ricardo.

"I have tried to explain it all to him," the old man was saying, "but I'm not sure how much of it is getting through."

"I think you're doing a great job," The Giant Fly said. "He's a tough subject, but he does think about everything you say."

"Well, he does bring me wine," the old man said, "so that makes it easier. Can you tell me again, if you'd be so kind, about how time flies? I always love hearing that story."

"Gladly," said The Giant Fly, "it's one of my favorites too. Basically, time moves at twice the speed of light. The best way to explain it is to look at electricity. Imagine you have a piece of copper wire. That copper is made up of electrons. If you apply electricity to one end, it feels like it instantly appears at the other end. But the electrons aren't moving— rather the electro-magnetic waves of the electricity are rushing past them, and the speed of those waves is at the speed of light."

"Exactly at the speed of light?" the old man asked.

"Well, it's slows down a bit because of the imperfection

of the copper electrons, so with copper maybe it's at seventy percent the speed of light, but if the pathway was perfect, it would be at the speed of light. Electricity, like light, is just an electro-magnetic wave... of course, I'm talking about the light you can see."

"And how fast is that again?" the old man interrupted.

"Visible light moves at approximately 186,000 miles per second," the Giant Fly said. "But suppose there was a different light, a light you couldn't see. It might move at a faster speed. It moves so fast you can't see it. That's what time is—it's a form of light, but faster. It moves at twice the speed of light we can see."

"Wow, that's amazing."

"If you had eyes like mine," said The Giant Fly, "you could see time. I can see it as it shoots by you."

"What color is it?" asked the old man.

"The closest color you have is green," said The Giant Fly. "Of course, that's just a metaphor. Color, after all is dependent on light, so a different light, like time, has a whole array of different colors."

"Wow," said the old man. "Different colors. I can't wait to tell Ricardo this."

"Well," said The Giant Fly, "try not to forget."

*   *   *

All of these things were occurring exactly at the same time as Ricardo was getting ready for bed, while he brushed his teeth, washed his face, and took his nightly blood pressure medicine. All these events were unfolding in other people's lives, completely unbeknownst to him.

As Ricardo got undressed and slipped into bed, his thoughts drifted back over his day. He remembered how he had awoken that morning, gone on his morning run, gotten the email from Carolina, made the trip to the bathhouse in La Chorrera, had dinner at the Soda de la Linda, gone to visit with the old man, and then had his Skype conversation with Carolina.

As Ricardo began to drift off to sleep, he wished again

he could do more for Carolina; he wished again he could see Marta; he wondered what had happened to Magali and to Ali; and he felt a sleepy sadness that he had just floated though his day.

"That's how life is," the old man had once told him, "we are simply floating on our little rafts, only aware of the planks that hold us afloat at that moment, completely unaware of the huge ocean of experience, memory, feeling, history, past and future that we floating on. It is an ocean of infinite depth, infinite horizon, and it makes up every single molecule of our existence on the raft—every bit of air we breathe, every smell of salt water we smell, every single wave we feel, every single thought we have. And we, the sick poor impoverished stupid creatures that we are, we are oblivious to everything at that moment, and every single moment of our existence, completely oblivious except for the few planks of our raft. If we could open our eyes and look beyond our raft, we could see our destiny, our course across the ocean, our death that right now awaits us, that has already consumed us, that is already rebirthing us, but of course we cannot. We are doomed to our rafts, our heads bowed, floating on the ocean of time, dumb and mute."

As Ricardo fell asleep, he began to dream. He began to dream of a time far in the future, and in his dream he was getting up from bed. He had been down with the flu for several days and had spent his time sleeping. But in his dream he was recovering, and he felt good enough to get up from the bed, and he felt good enough that he was thinking that maybe, just maybe, he would walk downtown and buy a bottle of Sangria.

-FIN-

ABOUT THE AUTHOR

Robert Rahula was born in Spain to an American father and Spanish mother, but grew up in Virginia on the farm of his paternal grandparents. He returned to Menorca, Spain, in the 1960s to pursue his writing career. These days he travels in Europe, Central and South America for several months a year, giving readings and lectures, and spends the rest of his time writing, dividing his time between Spain and the United States.

Over the past 30 years, Robert has published dozens books of prose and poetry in Spain and in the United States. While he remains relatively undiscovered in the United States, he is revered in Spain as the founder of the "portilla" style of popular Spanish poetry: non-metered fluid verse that deals with love, loss, bisexuality, separateness, and growing older.

All of Robert's novels are available in English, including his groundbreaking erotic novel *Messieurs*; his second English novel *Panamaniac;* his erotic murder mystery *Island of Misfits*; his acclaimed supernatural novel *One Last Fling;* his "sexistential" novel *Conversations in a Belgian Bar;* as well as his "Dan Landes Mystery" novels: *Bathhouse Stories, All the Yage in Reno, Exigent Circumstances,* and *Uninvited Guest.*

Eight volumes of Robert's English poetry are also available: *Trigger Points; Inside the Locked Heart; Camino; Migration; I Sing the Body Politic; Wonderland; From Whose Bourn; Expat Poems;* an anthology of his English poems and short stories, *Half-Life;* and a collection of his most famous Spanish poems, *Poemas Españoles.* Other poems, along with his blog on writing and his tour itinerary, appear on his Facebook page and on his website robertrahula.com

www.ingramcontent.com/pod-product-compliance
Lightning Source LLC
Chambersburg PA
CBHW071534100726
47908CB00004B/1390